FROM THE ASHES

FORBIDDEN SERIES: THE PREQUEL

DANI RENÉ

In order to rise From the Ashes
A Phoenix must first burn in the fire

PLAYLIST

Run - Snow Patrol
Hurricane - Thirty Seconds to Mars
End of All Days - Thirty Seconds to Mars
Hurts So Good - Astrid S
Stay - Rihanna, Mikky Ekko
Only Girl (In The World) - Rihanna
Dirty Dancer - Enrique Iglesias, Usher
Hurts - Emeli Sandé
The Kill - Thirty Seconds to Mars
Nights Like This - W. Darling
Bunny Park - Cnsrd, Laco
Ride - SoMo
Feels - Kiiara

PROLOGUE
Skyla

The lights are focused on us as we finish up our routine. The stages are in the center of a large lounge area and every man's eyes are glued to the two of us. We've become somewhat of a team. Men love my red hair and her chestnut locks. Her hazel eyes and my emerald pools seem to hypnotize them.

There are two platforms, mine which is off to the left has one sleek, silver pole, and to the right Dakota's has a chair, which she's currently leaning on as the song ends. Her long, slender legs shimmer with the glitter she brushed on earlier.

Inferno.

The nightclub that's given me a sanctuary from my past. An elite club with only the richest of clientele. They pay an exorbitant fee to see me wrap my legs around a metal pole. They watch me and the girls, sway and gyrate, wearing slinky outfits.

They beg us to taunt them.

For the more exclusive clients, there's a menu if they'd like more than just a dance. When they request something from that sleek silver card, we're at their beck and call.

From where I'm positioned backstage, I notice Dax, my boss, and Axel, the head of security—the only two men I trust since leaving the hell I came from—stalking toward the bar. They've been good to me and the other girls who work for them.

"Skyla,"—Dakota's melodic voice drags me from my daydreams of another life—"orders up!" she quips, with a smile so bright it lights up her face. I know what she means, two clients requested us. The VIP package in this place means men can ask for any girl to join them in a private room, and if they pay the premium, they get to fuck us, and it seems tonight Kota—which is her stage name—and I will be entertaining someone.

I follow my best friend down the hallway. "Which room are we in?"

She glances at the card that Theia gave her and responds over her shoulder. "The Raven Room, looks like we have two men to dance for tonight." This room is mine—well, it's my favorite. With muted colors and a beautiful pole in the center, I feel as if they made it for me.

Upon entering we find the clients already seated in the onyx wingback chairs. They're both older, possibly mid-forties. One of them has a thick gold band on his ring finger, glimmering under the low lights coming from the ceiling.

"What can we do for you gentlemen today?" I stop only a few feet from them, my red panties and bra leave little to the imagination. Dakota heads to the pole, twirling around

it hypnotically. I've been teaching her some moves and she's picking them up quickly.

"I'm Travis. This is Rich. He wants to watch, doesn't want to cheat on his wife," the one with salt-and-pepper hair says, gesturing to his friend. I almost laugh at that. Of course he doesn't. "I, on the other hand, would love to control you and your little friend," he quips, and I nod in understanding.

"You want a dirty show?" I question, meeting the steel gray eyes of Rich. His dark brown hair is just graying at the sides. He nods. No fucking shame. "Fine, make yourselves comfortable."

Since I've been at Inferno, Dakota's one of the girls I've grown close to, the other is our hostess, Theia. They've both been an incredible support after the horrors I faced. They're both honest to a fault, and love me even in my self-loathing moments.

I think we do that for each other.

After my escape from Caged with the help of Dax, I've gotten attached to my makeshift family. Now, here in the Big Apple, a year into our friendship, we're like sisters.

Dakota's dressed in a skimpy, blue baby doll negligee, which is so short and see through, it's pretty pointless. She might as well be naked. She gives me that sexy little pout that drives her clients crazy. Raising my finger, I crook it to call her over. When I turn back to the men, I find both clients are now shirtless, and for older men, they're toned in all the right places.

Without a word, Dakota heads toward me. Her tits bounce with every step and their eyes are glued to her. "This here is Kota, boys, and I'm Skyla." Two sets of eyes flit between us with eagerness. "Kitten, why don't you show these gentlemen how sweet you can be."

I reach for her arm and tug her against me. My chest against her back. We're standing in front of Travis as I reach for her tits, groping them, tugging and tweaking her pebbled buds.

"Isn't she pretty boys?" Rich is fixated on our display. My one hand travels down her flat stomach to find her bare little pussy. "Open your legs, K," she does and my fingers slip in easily. She's already wet and we've only just begun. I plunge two fingers into her, pumping them in and out. Her soft moans are the only sound in the room, until I hear the hiss of one zipper, then a second.

When I look at our audience, they've both got their dicks in their fists. Rich is smaller and not as thick, but the one who gets to play must easily be ten inches. That's going to hurt like a motherfucker. Pulling my fingers from her, I reach out to Travis. "Taste her," I murmur. He moves quickly, taking my fingers in his mouth and licking the sticky sweet juice from them.

"Fuck, that's delicious." He growls, then rises from the chair with his hungry gaze trained on us and shoves off the rest of his clothes. "I'm taking charge now. You're both going to lie down and obey." We don't argue because he doesn't look like he's joking.

His expression is something akin to someone who just hit the fucking jackpot. With two incredibly beautiful women doing as you wish, no man in his right mind could resist.

"Go sit on her face, pet. I think she needs to get a taste," he orders Dakota in a deep and rough tone. "Toys?" He turns to me, and I gesture to the chest of drawers. I know what he wants and he'll find them all in there. He pulls out the four thick leather cuffs and turns to the bed.

I lie back, watching him gawk as Kota's pert ass wiggles as she climbs on the bed. Rich is in awe staring at us as he strokes himself. She straddles my face and I immediately grip her hips, holding her against my mouth.

My tongue darts out, licking her smooth lips, tasting the sweetness of her honey. The moans that escape her are feral and sexy. The sound of sex is in the air and the scent of K's sweet little cunt has me salivating.

"Enough." The word rumbles between us. Her eyes are glazed as she glares at Travis. I know she was close, wet and primed. "Lie down, sweetheart. We'll make you feel better." We swap positions, and he goes to work using the cuffs to bind her to the bed. Her legs are spread wide and her arms are locked in place. No escaping now, little one.

She watches me and I offer a wink.

"I need to come, please?" she begs, but he ignores her.

"Soon," I whisper. Her plump lips part with a moan when he tugs on her nipple. Grabbing the ten-inch dildo, he joins us on the bed, and in my peripheral, I notice Rich has moved closer.

"First we're going to devour you." Travis's tone is filled with need. He hands me the clamps and I nod. He doesn't need any motivation. Leaning in, he licks and sucks her sweet flesh.

Her nipples are peaks and I set to work laving and teasing them. Once I've got them both wet, I use the metal clamps—which are attached to a thin metal chain—securing them to each taut bud.

Her soft mewls are evidence that she's aching for her orgasm. I've learned over the year that she's very much a little masochist. She thrives on pain and this has put her in her element. "Oh, please, please?" she pleads, and I almost feel sorry for her, but he's in charge. He reaches for the third clamp from my hand—the one I haven't yet used—and stares at her pretty eyes.

"Now," he orders, and pinches her clit with the metal teeth. Her body convulses and Travis's face is soaked in her release. "Good girl, so fucking sweet." He murmurs and licks every drop she's given him. His cock is rigid between his legs. With a quick glance at me, he commands in a deep tone, "I want you on her face while I fuck her." He grips his cock and I watch him rip the foil packet. "Sit on her face," he growls as he sheaths himself. I shift myself and straddle Dakota's pretty face. "Eat her cunt while I fuck you, little toy." I'm hovering over her mouth, and when her tongue darts out, it sends me spiraling. I grip the headboard and hold myself steady when I feel her sucking my hardened clit into her mouth. The pleasure shoots through my body, igniting my blood with a fire that races through my veins and I'm overcome with lust.

Her body is shoved up every time he thrusts into her, which in turn has my body convulsing without thought and my release detonates, bursting through me as I cry out.

"What a beautiful fucking sight," he murmurs, in awe of me and my best friend. "Get off her face. We're both going to fuck her." On wobbly legs, I move off Kota, her face glistening with my arousal. He slips out of her and I help untie her. "I want you on your back." He points at me, then turns to her. "You, little doll, will ride that plastic cock while I own your tight ass." Rich is now standing at the bed. His body is tense as his hand moves slowly over his erection.

I lie back, donning the strap-on with Dakota on all fours

over me. Her gasp as she sinks down on the dildo is a loud one. It's thick and I know it's filling her almost painfully. Pulling her over me, I watch her face contort as her puckered entrance is invaded by another solid intrusion. "Oh fuck, it's too much." Her whimper is soft and her eyes roll back in her head.

I latch on to her nipple, tugging the clamp with my teeth. I know the chain in turn tugs her clit and her body is now sandwiched between Travis and me. Suddenly, I feel the strap between my legs shifting and a dildo being teased into my pussy. Rich pushes it deeper. It's too much, too soon, when he starts fucking me with it.

We move in a rhythm that has fireworks shooting off behind my eyelids. My body convulses and spasms with the plastic cock inside me. When Travis hisses and spanks Dakota, her cries, his growl, and my own moans send me over and my orgasm grips me, sending me into outer-fucking-space.

Skyla

I've been imprisoned, trained, and then freed. Given a second and a third chance. Sometimes I don't remember the girl I used to be.

The one I was before my eighteenth birthday.

She's a distant memory.

Now, all that fills my mind are the images of what I've become.

Inferno has been my home for almost five years. When I escaped Caged, I found solace in this place. It's been a reprieve to have a choice in what I do. Dax told me I'm welcome to work the bar, or waitress, but dancing is something I love. Once I locked my demons up tight in a box, that I never want to visit again, I was happy with the freedom I gained.

There are times when I'm on stage and I wonder what my life would be like if I hadn't been taken, if I had gone to college to earn my Business Management degree. But I didn't get that chance. So, here I am, twisting around a metal pole, entertaining elite clients.

The club is beautiful, it's sleek, stylish, and sexy. The black and silver accents are startling against the blood-red sofas. Bright lights of all colors shine onto the two main stages. My podium has a long steel pole attached to it, and Dakota has her choice of apparatus.

She's been begging me to teach her some moves on the pole, but I know how addicting it is. Once you get started, you don't want to stop. I don't want her to live through the life I did, she's better than this, but somehow, I'm selfish. I don't want her to go because if she does, I'll be alone again.

So I do what I can. I teach her, show her, all because I'm afraid of losing someone again.

As I sashay over to the welcome desk, I take in Theia, our hostess, and boy does she dress the part. She reminds me of Zoey Deschanel, sexy, beautiful, and always dressed to kill. Her long, cocoa locks fall down her back that look like waves of chocolate. Her blue eyes—so similar to her brothers'—meet mine as I near her. "Skyla,"—she offers a friendly smile—"I'm busy setting up the schedule for next week. Do you want a full one, or were you taking time off?"

"Give me two days off, Wednesday and Thursday. I've got stuff to do uptown," I respond with a grin.

With an efficient nod, she responds, "You've got it, babe. Two days. Hope you have some fun." My heart sinks a little, I wish I was having fun. Dakota's working so I'll be on my own, but I've got paperwork to sort out.

With my mind on what I need to do, I'm lost in thought as I head down the long hallway past the VIP rooms. Some things that happen in there are better left unknown. "There's my favorite redhead." Axel's raspy growl startles me.

"Axe, what's up?" I question, turning to find a sinful smirk curling his lips. The man is something else. He's head of security for Inferno, and he's been like a personal bodyguard since I started here. With a body built like a brick wall, I feel safe when he's around.

"You joining me for lunch, Skyla?" he murmurs, and my name on his lips in that thick English accent definitely does have a tingle shooting down my spine. But after getting my heart broken and recovering from what I faced in my past, I've decided a man shouldn't be my focus, so I've steeled myself and locked my heart away.

"Is this a friendly lunch or are you trying to get yourself a date?" I quip, earning me a sexy grin.

He leans in, his mouth close to mine, but I don't flinch. "Baby girl, if I wanted a date with you, I'd get one," he tells me, confidence oozing from those full lips, "this is just a friendly meal where we can talk."

Talking.

I don't do that, he of all people should know that. I'm done letting people in. "Axe, as much as I love being around you, you know I'd never date you. But I can do lunch. Also, you should stop following me around." I giggle, and turn on my heel, forcing him to respond to my retreating back.

"I just like watching that pretty little ass sway in front of me, if only you'd let me get a taste." I can hear the smirk in his voice and there's a hunger there that sends a shudder through me.

"I don't fuck my friends, Handsome," I retort playfully before I'm out of earshot.

I pass my favorite room. The dark, decadent one with beautiful silvers and a four-poster bed that I don't mind being bound to, should a particular client enjoy that sort of thing. I've been through much worse than some rich boy playing Dominant.

Stopping at the dressing rooms, I pull open the door to find a few of the girls changing into their casual clothes. I've got two dances tonight and I need to get ready before the boss man walks in grouching at everyone.

I get settled at my vanity and start with my make up, a dark smoky eye is my favorite and I add the black liquid liner. Taking in my reflection, and the emerald eyes that are still so similar to my mother's, sends a wave of emotion lapping at me. My lace and silk lingerie is so different from the beautiful gowns I used to wear, that I wonder if I'll ever wear them again.

New York, my new home, is a city you can get lost in, which is what I wanted, needed. Working here has given me a new lease on life, I've got incredible friends and a job that pays well. Even though I've become accustomed to shaking my ass on stage, deep down I want a man to look at me like a woman again, not a doll, a toy, or a pet.

Don't get me wrong, I love what I do, but I *want* love. I really do. Somehow, I just don't see how it will happen. Only one man has ever held my heart, but he's no longer in my life.

I guess you could call us star-crossed, but with us there will be no second chances.

When I turned eighteen, my life took a turn and nothing I'd ever held dear would be within my grasp again. Then when I turned nineteen, my life changed again and since then I've had to find my footing in the real world again.

After losing everyone I ever loved—all the people I cared about—I shut down my heart. I hid myself in my depression. If it wasn't for Theia and Dakota, I'm not sure where I would have ended up. They've become like family, the sister's I never had, as well as Dax and Axel, who became the older brother's I always longed for.

I'm almost ready for work, just adding the final touches to my make-up, when I hear the knock on the door that tells me I'm being summoned. Adding the final touch of gloss to my lips, I'm ready for what the night is about to bring.

There's a party scheduled, although I'm not sure if it's a bachelor or birthday party, and I've chosen one of my favorite outfits. Thigh high black stockings clipped to a blood-red garter belt. The panties and bra are white silk—

soft against my fevered skin. I've just been waxed and my bare pussy feels like heaven against the fabric.

The crimson bow that adorns my bra and panties match the garter. White for purity and red for sin. My long red hair has been styled into large curls that cascade down to the middle of my back.

Rising to my feet, I step out of the dressing room and shut the door behind me. The backstage area is quiet, but I can hear the music booming through the walls.

Guess the party started early.

As I make my way to the bar, I find Theia talking to the staff. She's something else. Like an Energizer bunny, she's constantly moving through the club, making sure things are running smoothly. She and Dax make an incredible couple, both strong and independent, but deeply connected. He's been her Master for a long while and she's always gushing about how amazing he is as a partner.

Before I reach her, Dakota bounds up to me dressed in a beautiful black corset, the strings are pulled tight around her curvaceous torso, and her cleavage beckons. She grips my arm in excitement, like a kid at Christmas.

She's incredibly sexy. Her body is sinful and her mouth is wicked. I shake my head to clear my mind of the filthy thoughts of what she and I do when we're requested by clients.

"You're rather chipper tonight, Kota." I giggle, whispering in her ear using her stage name.

She shrugs nonchalantly, her hazel eyes meet my

emerald gaze. "I'm just excited, Dax said I can work with you tonight," she hisses, playfully leaning in and planting a soft kiss on my cheek.

"Ladies, can we keep that for the show?" Dax stalks up behind us, with a smirk on his lips and mischief dancing in gray blue eyes.

He's a good guy, someone who knows where we've come from and is willing to give us a chance to work and choose what we want to do. His body is an ink masterpiece, covering every inch of exposed skin down to his knuckles. Standing at almost six feet tall with muscles that always seem to bulge from his shirts, he looks as if he can kill with one hand. And I'm sure he can.

A trimmed beard adorns his chiseled jaw. With his long hair buzzed short on either side of his head, he reminds me of a tattoo artist rather than a businessman. Tonight he must have a meeting because he's dressed in a sleek Armani suit, looking every bit a mafia boss oozing professionalism.

"Sure, we're heading there now," I respond with a small smile, and he nods curtly, leaving us staring after his solid form.

"Jeez, someone's in a mood tonight," Dakota remarks, tugging me toward the private booths near the back of the club which clients can reserve for parties. These can comfortably seat thirty people, with two small stages as well as a bar. To these men money is no object, drinks flow, and the girls are tipped well.

There are two dancers for every fifteen men—we

dance, taunt, and tease, and they pay a shitload for it. Dakota and I are two of the four girls scheduled to entertain them tonight.

As soon as we step into the party area, I take note of the other two girls already on the small podium, swaying to the deep bass that vibrates through me.

I feel the hungry gazes on me. "Hey, sweetheart. You're beautiful," one of them whispers in my ear. His hand cups my ass, squeezing it hard, and I shudder, turning to find a face that doesn't look old enough to be in here.

"How about you finish your drink and we'll talk later," I wink, shoving his hand away. He smirks, holding up his hands in surrender and I turn to Dakota. "Is he even old enough to drink? Let alone be in here?" I hiss in her ear.

A giggle falls from her plump, shimmery lips, as she regards me. "You do realize you just asked the most innocent looking girl in this place if a client is old enough?" She's got a point. Dakota could pass as eighteen. Her sweet, angelic face is what always captures their attention, then when they notice she's built like a seductress, all bets are off. They'll throw money at her to see that pert little ass wiggling.

"Right, okay, Miss Babyface," I tease, and am rewarded with her beautiful smile.

"Let's mingle, I feel like a shot before we get up on that thing." She gestures to the stage, and I nod in agreement. A shot definitely sounds like fun. As we near the mobile bar, I notice the two jean-clad men at the one end. One has a charcoal shirt with the top buttons undone, the cuffs rolled up to his elbows. The sight of his tattoos has me grinning.

"Now we're talking, baby," I whisper. Dakota's gaze follows mine and we burst into a fit of giggles as we sashay up to the bar. The second guy has a light blue shirt on, and when they turn to regard us I'm startled by just how good looking they both are.

"Ladies," Charcoal Shirt says, in a tone that drips hunger. His gaze flits over me, then scans the little brunette beside me. His tongue darts out, wetting his full lips. I take in his friend and the intense gaze he's pinned me with holds me hostage. Searing gray eyes tempt me and I square my shoulders and meet his stare dead on, challenging him with a small smirk on my lips.

"Can we get you ladies a drink, or would you kittens like to take this"—he lifts the Cristal champagne from an ice bucket—"and go to one of the VIP rooms to play?"

"VIP costs extra," I counter, but his face cracks into a satisfied grin.

"I can afford it, darling. Don't ever doubt that," he returns confidently. Lifting his hand, he trails a slow, sensual path down my bare arm, causing chill bumps to dot every inch of my skin.

Lifting my mouth at the corner, I nod. Grabbing the bottle, I spin on my heel, hooking my arm through Dakota's. "Come on then, boys. Let's go," I say over my shoulder, and head toward the hallway where our private rooms are hidden away.

Blue Shirt follows me like a puppy ready to play and Charcoal Shirt has an over confident look on his face, as if he's just hit the jackpot.

"Raven Room?" I ask Dakota, and she nods with a little giggle. Whenever we're together, this is the one we favor. The four poster bed allows us to play with our cuffs and rope.

It's dimly lit and the soft glow of candles makes everything seem sexier. Allowing both men inside, I usher them toward the chairs. "My name is Beck," Charcoal Shirt says.

"I'm Skyla and my brunette princess here is Kota." I introduce her and she bounds into his lap. The man in the blue shirt stares at me and offers me a wicked grin. "Would you like a dance, or something a little more decadent?"

"Oh, definitely decadent, Red. I'm Jackson, and I'm going to enjoy you," he growls, and I put my hands on my hips, watching him. With slow precision, he unbuttons his shirt. He's not sculpted, but he's well-built. "Come here, I've been dying to see those red lips of yours at the base of my dick," he orders, and I drop to my knees. My partner in crime follows suit and soon we're both swallowing the men as we work in sync.

The only noises in the room are the dirty sounds of their grunts and our sexually charged, soft moans. Hands fist my hair, holding me in place, as Jackson's hips thrust up.

Suddenly, I'm dragged off his shaft, and when my eyes meet his, he winks. Pulling me up, he spins me around so I'm facing away from him. Hooking his fingers in the waistband of my panties, he drags them down my thighs. He bends me over and kicks my legs apart as two thick fingers probe my entrance. A grunt rumbles in his chest when he finds my wetness. "So wet, so fucking beautifully drenched. Come, sit on my dick."

Quickly, he sheaths himself and pulls me backward, allowing me to straddle him with my back resting against his bare chest. My legs on either side of the arm rests as he bounces me on his thick erection. Beck pops the champagne and orders Dakota to lick the bubbly liquid from my body as he slowly drizzles it between my tits. "Taste her sweetness with the champagne," he rasps.

Her hot tongue on my clit has my thighs trembling and as I gaze down, I find her face buried between my legs. Beck sheds his clothes watching the erotic scene before him. He positions himself behind my naughty girl and rolls on the condom before he drives his hips against her ass and by her moans, I'm guessing he's good at that. Four bodies moving in sync and the sounds that echo around the room are primal.

Sweaty skin. Grunts of pleasure. Moans of desire.

"You're so tight, kitten," Beck coos at my girl, "eat her pussy. I want to watch you lick his cock while he fucks her." Beck grunts and Dakota pushes her ass back against him. Her tongue laps at my pussy while Jackson slams into me. He has one hand around my throat, squeezing, and the other twisting and tugging on my nipples. An orgasm tightens low in my belly as heat floods my veins.

My blood is on fire and my clit throbs. "Fuck, your cunt is squeezing me. Make me come with that perfect little pussy, kitten." Filthy words echo around us, both men grunting and growling like rabid dogs.

"You feel fucking amazing, Red, take it. Every. Fucking. Inch," Jackson hisses, as his teeth sink into my neck, sending me spiraling into darkness as an orgasm shudders through me.

The squealing sounds of Dakota coming are enough to send me reeling into another earth-shattering release.

Kael

"On your knees, little one," I growl at her. She's turned eighteen and been given to me to train. There's no way to refuse. It's the family business, so I do as I'm told. Her body isn't as stick thin as the other girls. With womanly curves, no one would ever guess she's barely legal.

Her body trembles in the dank room. I'm sure she's close to freezing. Dressed in only a pair of skimpy panties, her breasts jut out, and I have to stifle my groan. I can't allow my emotions to get the better of me. All the girls are disposable. That's what my father—the head of the Wolfe household—has taught us.

"Please." Her soft plea sends desire coursing through my veins.

Heat burns my skin. Hunger boils deep in my blood.

As much as I hate this, the control and power I have over

them is enough to have me rock hard throughout the process.

The only rule—don't fall in love.

That's easy because this isn't dating. There are no feelings involved. It's purely sex. Lifting the rope by the pulley, I watch her arms stretch. She glances up. Big mistake. "Do. Not. Look. At. Me," I hiss. It's an order, but she's a feisty one. It's only her second day, but I know once the week is over, she'll be as submissive and obedient as a little kitten. Her eyes will be trained to the floor at all times, unless I order them up.

Stalking around her, I watch her tremble. The smooth skin on her back slowly dots with goose bumps and I smile because I know I affect her. I wanted to be an artist, but my father forbid it, telling me I'm a Wolfe, and I must accept my chosen path. So he dragged me into the fold.

It's been three long fucking years and here I am, Dominant or Master to five girls. This beautiful fiery one is my fifth. I have to get her ready for the shit that she's going to endure while she's working and living at Caged—the premiere underground BDSM strip club, where men come to fulfill their darkest and filthiest desires.

The things I've seen here are atrocities, but my father has contacts in law enforcement so they turn a blind eye. The clients we have are elite, well-known men—everyone from celebrities to politicians.

They all walk in here with the faded white circle on their ring fingers. Gold or silver bands hidden in shirt and jacket pockets until they shower and leave. Of course, they shower the filth off before they go home to their wives to have sweet, romantic, vanilla sex. You know the kind. The soft touches and

Grabbing my paintbrushes and palette, I stare at the canvas. It's blank, just like me. There's nothing coloring my world. My inspiration is in the fucking drain. A knock on my front door has me dropping the offending items and stalking to open it. As it swings open, I find my best friend on the other side.

"Hey man, what are you doing?" He ambles into the living space and flops onto my sofa. As soon as I shut the door, I join him.

I shrug my response. "Nothing, it's like my fucking brain and arm don't work anymore."

We both stare at the taunting white canvas.

"I know what you need." He jumps up suddenly and I stare at him expectantly. "A muse," he says easily, like I should have figured it out on my own. "You need a woman to bring you back to life."

I can't help chuckling. "Fuck off, man. That's the last thing I need. This contract is worth a shit load of money and I can't be fucking around. I need to work."

"Work? Are you actually working? You just told me you've got painter's block or some shit." He gestures to the non-existent painting I'm committed to finishing in three weeks' time, but it's not only that, I have another seven to finish over the coming six months, and I have no fucking idea what I'm going to do. "Why don't we head to Inferno? We can grab some drinks, check out some dancers with those spanking sexy asses," he quips, amused.

Narrowing my eyes, I cock my head to the side. *He can't seriously be thinking I'm going to head to that place.* "Why on earth would I go to Inferno with you?" I question slowly.

He stalks over to my kitchen area and pulls out two beers from the fridge. Snapping the caps off with the opener, he heads back to me and hands me one. I accept thankfully, taking a long draw. "Firstly, there are pretty women who shake their asses on stage and do all sorts of fun things backstage. Secondly, you need inspiration, and they have tons." Groaning, I roll my eyes at his suggestion and grab my remote control for the sound system. Thirty Seconds to Mars blares through the speakers. It's an old song—"The Kill"—but the lyrics resonate with me. They're about finding yourself, finding out who you really are.

These past five years have seen me lose my way. Become someone for everyone, but I know deep in my gut I'm not happy. How can I be when I killed someone? Maybe not her body, but her soul? My greatest fucking achievement, I think with remorse choking me.

"What have you got to lose?" I stare at Axel.

He's serious.

What have I got to lose?

Not much. I don't have anything anyway.

The image of *her* flits through my mind again, but I push it down. The one woman I loved yet could never have. I glance at my friend and nod. "Fine." He looks like a kid at Christmas who just got told he's getting a brand new bike.

"Fuck yeah!" He lifts his bottle, clinks it against mine, and downs every drop of liquid. "So, how about you meet me there tonight?" He chuckles and I nod. There's no way I can refuse him. He won't give up until we are sitting front row watching some chick shake her ass. "I need to jet, but I'll see you later, yeah?" Nodding my head, I push up from the sofa as he leaves my apartment like he owns the goddamn place.

After I left Caged, I found myself in New York trying to start the business I always wanted—painting, being an artist. It's been tough to forget what I witnessed in that place, but the biggest regret I have was losing *her*. Finishing my beer, I head into my room to pull on a decent looking T-shirt, a pair of black ripped jeans, and pull my long hair into a bun. It's been years since I last laid eyes on her, but she's so deeply embedded in me that I remember every curve, each beauty spot that adorned her skin, and I remember her taste. That sweetness she gifted me with all those times.

Only, she didn't know me. I'd never taken the mask off. I couldn't because I knew that if I ever got to see her again, I didn't want to see the hate in her eyes from what I did to her. My heart stutters at the thought of seeing that face, looking into those eyes. I wish she'd walk into my life and tell me she loves me. That the month we had wasn't just training. It was real.

Shaking my head, I make my way out of my apartment. If I'm going out tonight, I suppose I should get some new jeans and a shirt. The sun beats down on me as I head to my Wrangler. Jumping into the drivers' seat, I head out to the the main highway and toward the mall with thoughts of *her* on my mind.

"This is going to be epic, I'll get you a private dance." Axel smirks as we walk into the club. He's been working here for as long as I remember. I met him after I left Caged and our friendship has strengthened as the years moved on.

Even though I've never set foot in this place, he's never once questioned me about it. Accepting that I was still in love with someone else, he allowed me to wallow in self pity and when he had a day off, he'd swing by mine with beers and we'd get drunk talking about random shit.

Nearing the welcome desk, a pretty woman with long, chestnut waves, dressed in a tight fitting bright pink tank top, glances up and offers Axel an eye roll, but me a small, shy smile. She's beautiful, innocent looking, yet elegant.

"Axe, it's your night off and you decide to spend it

here?" She grins at him, then turns her attention on me, "have you been here before?"

"No, Kota, this is his first time in our fine establishment." Axel responds before I can and I chuckle at my best friend's flirting. She grins, but shakes her head at him, then pulls out a card, handing it to me.

Not responding to his advance, she pins me with a curious stare and explains the rules. "Well, you have a choice. Either you can stay and watch the main floor entertainment, or perhaps if you're willing to put down some serious cash, you're welcome to order anything off the cards." She points a manicured finger at the silver paper in my hand.

"Thanks, we'll check out the main floor," I respond curtly, and she offers a smile that's too innocent for where she's working. Tugging on my best friend, we make our way to the bar.

"Two beers, please?" I ask the bartender, who gives me a nod and grabs two bottles from the fridge. Once I've paid, we head to the tables around a small square stage which has a sleek, silver pole attached to it. The music fades and the lights dim. "Is Theia working tonight?" I ask my best friend and he shakes his head. My sister helps run Inferno. Even though I left home five years ago, I kept tabs on my brother and sister. I'm about to ask him when she'll be here, but I'm interrupted by a spotlight on stage and the voice of the emcee.

"The next lady on stage tonight,"—the sultry voice that comes from the speakers grabs my attention—"is one of the favorites. She's a beautiful fiery Goddess who definitely knows how to work the pole. Skyla is all yours, gentlemen." The announcement ends and the emcee steps off the stage. There are only men in the room and they start whistling for this girl. I sit back and when a single white spotlight shines down on the steel pole, she steps up onto the stage.

My gaze travels slowly up long, lithe legs, to a skimpy crimson lace thong, which hugs what I can tell from my front row seat is a smooth pussy. I let my gaze drift higher and find a torso made for sin, licking my lips, I take in the Phoenix tattoo on her ribs and my heart stutters wildly. When I reach a pair of perfect tits, hugged by red lace my cock jolts, but it's only when I meet familiar emerald eyes, that my heart stops completely. *Fuck. Shit.*

My breathing is ragged and my grip on the bottle is so tight, I'm sure I'll shatter it if I don't calm down. *Skyla.* Her long red hair hangs in loose waves, framing her incredibly beautiful face with porcelain skin.

The song starts and I recognize it as "Dirty Dancer," this version is sung by famous, Dutch symphonic metal band, Within Temptation. She spins around, gripping the metal as she moves her body hypnotically. Her legs wrap around the shimmering pole and I'm enraptured by the beauty that is her.

Paige Madden, the love of my life.

The woman I wanted to marry one day.

The one I walked away from because I didn't have a choice.

"I want her, a private dance," I hiss at my best friend, and his gaze darts to me in surprise.

"Really? You want little Red?"

Rolling my eyes, I nod. "Yes, I've never been so sure of anything in my whole life." Even though I've told him about a woman I once loved, I never told him anything more. Having to talk about her was pain enough, so I hid everything from him.

I watch her move, sway, spin, and my blood heats with desire and need. She slides down the pole with practiced precision, her feet touch the stage and she moves in front of the pole.

Glistening eyes dart around the room as she kneels before us. She meets every man's gaze, until hers falls on mine.

Time stops.

The lights dim.

Music fades.

And it's just us.

Two strangers. Two lovers.

A man and a woman who know nothing more than pain.

Agony so profound, so fucking brutal, that nothing can take it away.

Only each other.

As my gaze lingers on her face and I meet those familiar eyes that are so green I feel as if I'm staring into a forest, my heart stops. My chest heaves as I try to take in life giving breath, but the only thing I need to survive is her. Not one taste, not two, but a lifetime.

She's changed somewhat—sexy, confident, sensual.

It's her.

Pushing off the chair abruptly, I head to the pretty little hostess. Her eyes dart up to me in surprise as I stalk closer and when I reach the desk, I'm out of breath, not from exertion, but from the sheer need for the woman with the red hair. "Can I help you?" she questions curtly.

"Yes, yes, I need a private room with the girl that's on the pole stage right now."

She gifts me a soft smile and nods. "That's Skyla, I'll let her know she's been booked. Any particular room?" she asks, but I don't care. All I need is time alone with her so I shake my head. "And you'd like the VIP package?"

"What does that entail?"

"Sex. She's one of our premier girls, she's got a list of limits, which you'll receive when I give you the room key. That allows you to see what she's not willing to do." I nod. Sex. With her. God.

"Yes." I slide over my black credit card and her lips quirk in a knowing grin that this piece of plastic holds no limit. "Any cost. Charge it to that card." She lifts the plastic and swipes it on the machine. Waiting for the approval— which I know will come easily—is brutal punishment because all I can think of is being alone with my firebird, my fucking Phoenix.

As soon as it prints my receipt, she hands me a black key tied with a red silk ribbon and a business card attached to it. "This is the key and a card for the fiery vixen, it will have her list of limits which is important for you to read through." She grins, and pushes up from her chair. "I'll escort you to the Raven Room."

"Thank you." As my smile meets hers, my heart thuds painfully. I pull out my phone and send Axel a message. His response is what I expected. *Have fun.*

"You can wait in the room. She'll be here a few minutes after she's finished her routine." With that, I'm left alone with a black door and a key to my future. As soon as I unlock the door and step inside, the scent of patchouli hits me. It's her. Everything about her.

Lifting the card from the silk ribbon, I read her limits. She's into being bound, spanked, and collared. Of course. I'll collar her soon enough.

My eyes dart around, almost nervously, taking in the lack of color in this room—it's elegant, just like her.

Three walls are black, and the fourth one is made entirely of windows that overlook the city. The view is spectacular, but the only thing I want to stare at is her.

A jet-colored metal four poster bed, with tufted, black wingback headboard sits against one wall and I'm already envisioning her bound to it. The bedding is gray, with a faux fur throw, the four pillows are white cotton, and I'm guessing the sheets are white as well.

The rest of the furniture is all muted tones—charcoal and silver.

As an artist, color is important, but she's so alluring that I'll gladly leave the shades, hues, and tints to spend time in her monochrome world.

Not long after I settle in one of the wingback chairs, the door opens and she strolls in. Her confidence falters and I fear she's recognized me somehow. I know it's not possible, but my mind is reeling from seeing her here, in the flesh.

"Skyla?" Her name rolls off my tongue. It's a question, one she doesn't answer. Her fiery red hair and those beautiful jade pools have me hooked. How she ended up here is a mystery I'm about to uncover.

I'm out of my depth because I've never paid for sex. And even as she offers me a flirtatious look, there's something hidden behind the sultry smile that makes me want to watch as she comes apart under my touch.

I want to see the expression on her face when fierce desire and violent passion slowly unravel her.

She steps forward, dressed in a one-piece bodysuit made entirely of lace. She's changed her outfit and I wonder if she does so for all her clients who request VIP. Even though the material is sheer, it hides what my mouth waters to see again.

She's still got those beautiful curves—hugged by the soft black material—and her cleavage teases me from where I'm sitting. When I finally rise, I hope my jeans hide the erection behind my zipper.

Long toned legs taunt me in four-inch black pumps, and I imagine fucking her with those heels digging into my ass. Pulling me closer.

"Before we start, there are few things I need to know," she says in a confident tone that has a hard edge to it. Even so, it still has a softness which is a stark contrast with her appearance.

I notice as she moves closer, the only vibrant color in this room is her fiery red hair. She stands out amongst the darkness like a flame.

"What do you need to know?" I inquire.

She gestures to the chair and offers a smile, which doesn't reach her eyes. It's practiced, like she's been doing this her whole life, and that saddens me.

She crosses her arms in front of her, which in turn lifts her breasts, but she's so confident in herself that she's making me throb. Even more than when she was a shy girl. Her gaze settles on me with her perfect lips pursed in a tight line. "Your kinks. There'll be no weird shit like watersports of any sort. If you want to take a piss, the toilet is over there." She points to the door where I guess the en-suite bathroom is. "No blades or any of that strange kink. You want to tie me up, go ahead, you want anal, I'm your girl." Her voice is rigid, like she's trained herself not to show fear. She settles in the chair beside me, her gaze never straying.

Nodding, I sit back and absorb her beauty—that sensual allure she moves with. "I'm not into any *weird shit*, as you put it, firebird." I respond, throwing her words back at her and adding in something I know she'll recognize— the nickname. Her brows shoot up at my words.

"Firebird?"

I nod, meeting her intense gaze. "Yes, you're as alluring with that red hair as a Phoenix," I answer honestly, then continue, lowering my voice, "like you've been reborn from the ashes." Because she has.

She drops her arms, relaxes her posture and regards me almost quizzically before asking, "And what makes you think I didn't die in the fire?" Her question is a brutal reminder of her past, a part of her life she doesn't realize I know about because she'll never recognize me. There's no answer I can give her right now because if I do, she'll know.

"Why don't we play and then I'll tell you?" I counter, and she nods with a small grin, quirking those beautiful lips. Pushing up from the chair, I watch as she walks over to the bed without a backward glance.

She crawls onto the soft comforter, and when she reaches the pillows, she lies back and regards me. Prey waiting for the predator to devour it. Taunting and teasing.

Temptation is something I've never been able to say no to, and this time is no different. I unbutton my shirt, allowing it to slip from my shoulders, and drop it on the chair. Meeting her gaze again, I unbuckle my belt, and pull it from the loops. Her green eyes are fixated on me as if we've swapped roles and now I'm the hunted.

"It says on your card that you love being bound. I take it you'll obey my orders as well?" My raspy tone is evidence that my restraint is faltering and I'm hanging on by the tips of my fingers.

"Yes, Sir," she murmurs playfully, and I'm ready to test that theory.

"Don't address me as Sir just yet, firebird. A man

needs to earn your submission," I respond, confidently this time. I want her to want to be mine, but not because I'm paying her for it.

"Okay." Her response is short and I hear the shock lacing it.

I push my jeans off and once I'm down to my boxer briefs, I stalk toward her, gripping my leather belt. Her gaze falls to it and then trails up to meet my eyes. "You like pain?" she asks, in a soft submissive voice.

That's my girl.

"No, I like control," I growl, and she nods. "Kneel and lower that top. I want to see your tits." And just like I know she's trained to do, the switch happens and she obeys.

Skyla

His order shudders through me, and my submissiveness surfaces. It's been five years, and I'm still a trained pet. The control he oozes reminds me of someone, reminds me of heartbreak and love all wrapped up in a beautiful package. The only difference is this man is inked like a masterpiece, whereas *he* wasn't.

Shaking my head to clear my mind of his overwhelming presence. I drop to my knees and reach up to undo the ribbon of my bodysuit. His heated gaze penetrates me, but it's filled with reverent emotion, unlike the hunger I normally see on client's faces. I'm confused at how he can come across like a dominating force, yet still be polite and sweet.

He hasn't smiled and I have a feeling if he does I may

combust.

The man is beautiful, fucking gorgeous to be honest.

His long honey-colored hair is tied into a messy bun. The beard he's wearing is tidy, sexy, and I wonder how it would feel between my thighs. His body is toned, but lean with a beautiful set of abs. V muscles point to a thick, hard erection and I rake my gaze over his toned thighs. Every inch of him is perfect.

Dark brown, almost black, eyes hypnotize me. The familiarity of them brings back the ache in my chest for a moment and I almost want him to turn away, but I feel like I not only want his gaze on me, I need it on me.

Only two men in my life have called me firebird, or Phoenix, one I've blocked out mentally because when he walked out he left me a shattered girl.

The other, was the one who made me accept my future, but the client before me is neither of those. Even so, when he called me firebird my heart catapulted because just for a moment, I wished with everything I have that he could be my savior.

It unnerves me how this stranger can see into my soul.

Once I'm naked, he'll see just how well he read me.

I'm bare from the waist up and his hungry stare drinks in every inch of me. My nipples harden under his intense scrutiny. "You're perfect." The words wash over me, but they don't purify me. I don't believe them because there's no sanctity for me. I'm far from perfect, in fact.

What man could want, or even love me? Even the man I believed did, walked out on me.

"Are we going to get this show on the road?" My snarky question earns me that long-awaited smile and it's just as I imagined it would be—drop dead fucking gorgeous. It's a boyish, crooked grin with dimples forming on either cheek.

Once he's taken his fill of my presentation position, he pins me with a glare that holds me hostage. "Take off that scrap of material you call underwear, or I'm going to rip it off with my fucking teeth," he growls, and it's the sexiest thing I've ever heard. I rise and push the rest of my bodysuit off, and when it falls to the floor, I settle my gaze on him, awaiting his command. "Lie back, spread those beautiful legs, and get your cunt wet."

His filthy words send shockwaves through me. Those dark eyes seem to see me as more than a dancer, they look through me and my body quakes with a powerful need and again, I'm reminded of someone else. I blink hard to rid him from my mind, I need to keep my focus on the job.

Men have always spoken to me like I was nothing more than a pet to use, but only one has made me want to obey as much as this sex god standing before me.

The gruff growl so familiar, the stance every bit as commanding, and the fuel that burns me from the inside, makes my body quake. His grip on the belt turns his knuckles white, and I watch in awe as his other hand grips his cock through the tight black material of his underwear.

With two fingers, I tease my sex, opening the smooth lips to his hungry stare. The need to tease him, to show him how much I actually want him, runs through my veins like a current, setting me alight. Dipping one digit inside my body, I find that I'm soaked, slick with desire for a man who's acting like *he* used to and I'm not afraid. I want it.

The air around us is heavy with passion and desire, with emotion, which leaves me aching, needy, as if he's about to shatter me like glass and I would willingly let him.

"Fuck," he growls. The word sounds menacing. Like a threat, and I want to see him follow through, so I continue my teasing. Plunging two fingers inside me while my other hand teases and tweaks my hard nipples, my body bows off the bed and I feel my release coiling like a serpent readying itself to strike.

A soft moan falls from my lips like a siren's song, taunting him, calling to him to show me what he can do to my body, my mind. An unbidden thought comes to mind—I want him to breach my high walls and find my heart. This hope scorches me and strangles me with its force. The images of *that* place creep into my mind and I remember him as if he's standing before me. As if he's the one about to ravage me. And I want it. I want him. I need him.

"Stop." Immediately my hand falls away from my pussy and I'm jolted back to reality with a sudden force, as I lock my gaze on his. He wants to control my orgasm. I was a slave for long enough to recognize the need in his voice. "On your knees. I want to see you from behind."

Quickly, I move onto all fours and wait. A harsh swat

on my ass has me whimpering. For years I've enjoyed rougher, harder sex and he has me craving it right now. My body trembles for him. "So beautiful," he murmurs, so softly I'm sure I imagined it. I await the next sting, but it doesn't come. Instead, two thick fingers slide into my drenched sex. "Fuck my fingers, Phoenix, make yourself come."

His tone is raspy, and I do as he says. Pushing back, I ride his hand like I would his cock.

Fast, hard, and deep.

I feel him twist both digits inside me, and when he crooks them, hitting my G-spot, I fly apart. "That's my beautiful firebird. Soar for me." His words, along with the way he's rubbing my inner walls, have my body convulsing.

Memories mixed with the *here and now* assault me like a wave crashing harshly on the shore and I break, I shatter for him. Tears sting my eyes, but I blink them back. He's just too familiar and I'm not sure I can do this, but I have to, it's my job.

As my breathing evens and my heart rate slows, I feel fingertips tracing the ink on my ribs and hip. "You have risen from the ashes, more beautiful than ever before." Something in his tone, in the words he utters, has my body alert. And once again I'm hit by the surety that he knows me.

It can't be him. *He* left me.

Alone and cold to fend for myself in the horror that followed.

Once he pulls his fingers from my core, I turn to face him in time to see him lick my arousal from both digits. Our gazes lock and something shifts between us, a palpable force that knocks me breathless for a moment and as much as I want to ask him, I don't. Fear overrides the need to know. An inexplicable, invisible connection seems to tether me to him. At that moment, there's nothing I want more than to feel him inside me. "I want you." The words tumble from my lips in a soft plea. I've never asked a man to fuck me. Never willingly begged a man to take me, but I've just done it.

I lie back wanting to watch his face while he fucks me. Without a word, he shoves his briefs down thick, muscled thighs. His hard cock stands proudly, and I watch him rip the foil packet—I didn't even notice him holding—and sheath himself.

"Where would you like me, baby?" The question stills my heart and my belly flips with an unknown feeling. I'm not used to men being accommodating. I prefer them taking me without restraint. No emotions. Don't fall. Don't get hurt.

"Wherever you'd like?" I respond quietly, still in awe of him. My gaze trails over his tanned, taut skin, trying to see through the tattoos that adorn his body, to find the man hidden beneath. To find *him*.

He grips my hip with one hand and with the other he teases my entrance with the tip of his erection.

"Are you ready for me?" he grits out, his tone filled with hunger, and I nod. That's all he must need, because his hips slam into me and I'm suddenly filled beyond all imagination. My body quivers and my back arches off the bed. My heart thuds hard against my chest as he thrusts into me.

The hold he has on my body tightens. I'll be bruised, but I don't care.

He's made me feel more like a woman than anyone else before and something inside me snaps.

"Just fuck me," I cry out, needing something harder, rougher, more volatile because he's going to break through every fucking barrier I've built and do something no one else has done in a long time.

He's going to make me feel.

He reaches down and grips my neck, squeezing just enough to make my heart race. My eyes flutter closed before I hear the buckle and await the pain. But there isn't any. All he does is wrap the belt around my neck, pulling it like a leash as he bucks into me.

The crown of his dick rubs against my sweet spot over and over again. "You're so perfect, so fucking tight, firebird. You love it rough, don't you?" I try to nod, but the belt is too tight. I've been choked before, but it's never turned me on like it does now. My walls tighten around his thick shaft and I hear his feral growl. "Fucking beautiful, your tight cunt fits me like a glove." His words are dirty, downright filthy, but they detonate me.

An orgasm shatters through me and I cry out as my body spasms around him. His body shudders and I feel him thicken, joining me in bliss. It's silent for a long while, and once another beat passes, I watch his mouth curl into a lazy smile. "Perfect, firebird," he whispers, as he slips out of me.

I feel empty without him inside me and when I peer up, I find him staring at me with too much emotion.

"There's an en-suite if you'd like to freshen up. I'll tidy the room," I offer. He stalls for a moment, and I wonder if he's going to stand there all day. His mouth opens to say something, then closes again and he heads to the bathroom.

Shutting my eyes, I take a deep breath.

That was strange. Our connection.

I've never *wanted* a man since the one who holds my heart. Yes, I've fucked loads of men. If you asked me how many, I couldn't tell you, but this was different. It's as if he'd struck a match, and I'm the wick that now burns. A live flame.

Kael

As soon as I'm alone, I take a deep breath. There's no way she recognized me, but there was something in the way she looked at me, as if her soul recognized mine, her heart saw right through and found mine, beating wildly to the same rhythm.

Never did I think I'd see her again. Yet, here she is. I've just been inside her and her body still molds to mine like it was made to. As if we're one. I stare into the mirror, my eyes glazed with hunger, need, and love. Love so fucking strong I don't know how I'm going to go back out there and not tell her.

She's fucking beautiful. Perfect in every way. I knew she would be.

The words tattooed on her ribs and the Phoenix on her hip are evidence that she remembers.

I want her. I need her.

I have to decide if I should tell her the truth now, or wait. Show her that I do love her. She needs to know me, the real me.

Opening the shower door, I turn on the taps and wait for it to heat up. My mind is running rampant, formulating a plan to win her back. Once I step inside, I allow the spray to cascade down my tense muscles.

Sex is supposed to calm me, but it's fucking wound me up and I'm ready to snap. Every nerve in my body is alight, sparking like a live wire. I wanted to fuck her without a barrier, to feel her heat on mine, skin on skin. Soon, I will take her and claim her as mine.

I've waited too long for this—she'll wear my mark and only mine.

She's by no means innocent, but I'm fucked because all I want to do is defile her.

Gripping my dick, I stroke it. I'm rock solid and I've just come.

The ache to fuck her again is strong as it courses through my body, tempting me like a drug shot directly into the vein that ignites my blood.

"You need help with that?" Her soft, but confident tone has me turning to face the most beautiful woman I've ever seen. She's standing in the doorway of the shower, leaning against the wall, watching me with a smirk that makes me want to fuck those plump lips. Her body is still bare and I turn to face her fully.

"You offering?" I chuckle. She shrugs and the action

has her full tits bouncing. "Well, don't just stand there. It's not going to stroke itself," I order, and she immediately obeys, stepping into the shower. I bite back a groan when the spray hits her beautiful body. Those curves are like a roadmap for my tongue and I'd happily get a speeding ticket licking them.

"You're insatiable," she murmurs, dropping to her knees. She swirls her tongue over the tip of my dick, and I have to grip the wall to keep from coming too soon. Her gaze trails its way up my body, and when it finally reaches my eyes, the sparkle in those green orbs shimmer like jewels. She pulls her mouth off my dick and whispers, "I shouldn't do this."

My brows crease in a frown, but before I can ask what she means, the goddess rises and turns with her back to me. Bending at the waist, she grips the tiles in front of her. With those incredible forest pools, she glances over her shoulder and purrs, "Please, fuck me again."

My body responds, hardening further. I grip her hips and slam into her so hard, I hear the breath whooshing from her lips. She's incredibly wet and tight, making my cock thicken inside her hot body, aching to release and fill her. "Fuck, you're amazing," I grunt, and she whimpers in response. Her fingers claw at the wet, slippery tiles as I drive into her faster and deeper.

My hips slap against her ass and I bury myself so fucking deep inside her, it's as if we're one person. Joined in a primal dance. "Oh God, please..." She moans louder with every thrust.

Her curves set me on fire and her cunt clamps down on me. "Kael," I hiss through my teeth. "Scream my fucking name." My rough growl sets her off and her body quivers around me.

"Kael, fuck, please." Her words are a whimper, and I feel her orgasm closing in. Reaching around, I find her clit, pinching it hard between my index finger and thumb, sending her spiraling. "Oh fuck, Kael!" Her screams are primal, and my body locks as I shoot jet after jet of hot release inside her.

As I come down from the intense high, my hands still hold onto her like she's my lifeline. Which she is. I've lost her once, I'd rather die than lose her again. "Fucking hell, gorgeous. You aiming to kill me?" I question, chuckling as I slip out of her.

I watch those long legs tremble as she straightens and turns to me. "Just making sure you're happy with the service." Her words are cold, withdrawn.

Automated and robotic.

I reach for her and whisper a response. "Hey, I—"

She doesn't meet my eyes but instead interrupts me. "You better finish up. You'll need to return the key to the welcome desk. Take care." Without another word, she steps out of the shower and leaves me speechless under the cooling spray.

What the fuck?

Staring at the blank canvas, I pick up my paintbrush and palette. My hand moves of it's own accord. Inspiration blinks like a flickering light bulb as I start the painting. This contract is worth millions and I've been sitting here for two hours with one image in my mind. *Her.*

Nothing could have prepared me for what she's done to me. Seeing her beautiful face again has given me a new lease on life. If she knew who I was, she wouldn't have given me a second glance. There was so much anger in her eyes, not directed at me, even though it should be, but just anger at life.

I've seen her happy. Those beautiful eyes that used to shimmer and glisten have been dimmed over the years. Five long years. It's been too long.

My heart has beat for hers, and now that I've felt her again, there's no chance she'll get rid of me. Sitting back, I take in the crimson paint, which represents her hair, those long wavy locks that I want to wrap around my fist while I drive into her again and again.

The soft orange shades in between the dark red remind me of the sun shining down on her. Even though I've never spent time with her outdoors, I can picture her perfectly.

Smooth, creamy skin, plump pink lips, deep green eyes.

A Goddess.

A firebird.

A Phoenix.

The paintbrush sweeps along the white material as I

allow her to take over my mind. Memories flood me like a fountain overflowing. For the first time in years, I feel happy. It's an emotion I've lived without for so long, it startles me.

I'll go back tomorrow. Every fucking day if I have to. I want her. She'll be mine again. This time there's nothing standing in our way.

I promised you once I'd find you, firebird. Now that I have. I'll bind you to me so you'll never be on your own again. All I can do is hope and pray she forgives me. If not, I'll have to prove myself, which I'll do happily. I'll do anything she asks of me.

Watch out, Phoenix, I'm coming for you.

Skyla

Pushing open the door to our apartment, I notice it's dark. Dakota must be asleep. She finished work early, whereas I had a private dance scheduled. When I walked out of the Raven Room it was as if I left my heart there and I don't know why.

There was something about Kael I wanted more of. More of how he made me feel. Heading straight to my bedroom, I flop on the bed and stare at the black ceiling with my mind reeling.

Kael. I murmur his name, over and over again. The familiarity of him was so intense. Feeling him inside me was different, clients fuck us girls all the time, but with him, I ached for it. Begged for it.

As much as I wanted to ask him, to see if my suspicions

were right, I didn't. I chickened out. It couldn't possibly be *him*. I walked into the shower hoping to tempt him, to make sure he returns to the club, but nothing in life is certain.

Nothing would make him want more than just a quick, hassle-free fuck. Rolling over, I pull the sheet up over me and allow my eyes to flutter closed as dreams envelop me in their rigid claws.

"You'll fucking obey me, toy." His voice booms in the small room. I'd hoped I'd get a reprieve from him today, but sadly, I'm not that lucky. I drop to my knees on the black carpet and keep my eyes trained to the floor. The metal leash he always carries gets clipped to the collar around my neck. "Come." On all fours, I follow him, crawling like the pet I am. After the first year, I got a new Master to please. He's more violent, different from the one who trained me when I first arrived.

As we weave our way through the mansion, I know where we're headed. The music from the party room echoes down the hallway and as we near it, I can hear the men's voices over the deep thumping bass.

He's having a party again. Tonight, I'll be used until I pass out, maybe even after. I never remember how I get to my bed after these parties, but I always do. And without a doubt, I won't be able to walk for a few days.

"Well, what do we have here?" A deep rumble cuts through my thoughts and a hand, rough and calloused, reaches for my chin, tugging it up harshly. "She's a pretty one," he says to my owner, but stares at me.

"She's well trained," my Master says proudly, and I shiver. His voice is slurred, and I realize he's drunk already. "Come on, pet. Up on the table." He tugs the leash, pulling me toward the low mahogany table in the center of the room. I climb up with ease and sit back on my heels, waiting for my next command. The stranger who called me pretty crouches beside the table and meets my gaze. He's got kind blue eyes. I say kind, but what I really mean is that he's not scary. Not like my Sir.

"Do you like to play, little toy?" he asks, his tone laced with lust. All men talk to me like that.

I'm just a pet. A toy to play with.

"Yes, Sir," I mumble. He reaches out and tugs at the clasp of my bra, unhooking it with one hand. The straps fall to my front, and when the material drops from my body, I hear the loud hiss from the others. I don't know how many there are, but I would guess the usual six.

"So polite. Let's see how much that mouth can take." He rises, leaving me with a view of his shoes. They're shiny and black and remind me of the ones my father used to wear to work. The clink of a belt buckle alerts me that I'm about to be taken and it won't be nice. "Eyes up." Lifting my gaze, I watch as he unzips his expensive slacks and drops them to his knees.

The thick ridge of his erection protrudes in my face and I realize he wasn't wearing underwear. His big hand fists his shaft, taking the tip and running it over my lips. "Open your pretty little mouth, kitten." I obey, like I was taught to do, and he slips the crown of his dick in my warm, inviting, wet mouth. "Fuck." He grunts in satisfaction. "Suck it like you do those lollipops you girls like so much." My cheeks cave in as I swallow him, sucking harder. His groan is evidence that I've been trained well.

He grips my head, fisting my long, red hair in thick fingers, and plunges himself deep down my throat. My gag reflex kicks in and I choke on the tip as it hits me painfully. Spit drips from my chin and my eyes tear up. "Eyes up." Dragging my watery gaze up to him, I find a dark smirk on his lips.

As he continues fucking my face, I feel hands on me, ripping my panties from my curvy frame and groping my flesh. The man before me grunts and his body locks and jets of release fill my mouth. When he finally pulls himself from between my swollen lips, I'm dragged to the floor, and made to straddle a man with a mask on his face. I'm impaled on his thick cock and his hips rock up toward me as he fucks me bareback.

Just when I think I can't take anymore, another man nudges my tight, puckered entrance. Teasing it. I hear and feel the spit on my ass, and before the pain sears me, I retreat into my mind. The darkness I hold on to envelops me as I attempt to keep myself sane. As I try to grasp my soul and shield it from the filth and darkness, I pray for escape, beg for mercy, and plead for a reprieve.

"Just a toy, that's all you're good for. All you'll ever be."

Jolting upright from the nightmare, I glance around and realize I'm not there, I'm home. Safe. The images sit heavily in my mind, like a weight bearing down on me. I need to get out. To breathe. The air in my room is stifling.

I swing my legs over the bed and make my way in to the kitchen. The sun is coming up and I stifle a groan.

I'm not ready for another day. I'd prefer to sleep in, but I know I'll get no rest. "Good morning, sunshine!" Dakota's sweet, melodic voice comes from my right as she enters the kitchen. I glance at her happy face and sigh.

"Babe, do you have to be so chirpy in the morning?" I grumble playfully, and she smiles at my grumpy pout shaking her head. I swear the girl has a neverending supply of energy. Rounding the island, she grabs two mugs and proceeds to make us two steaming mugs of coffee.

"Here, drink this and lighten up, you're teaching me that damn pole today." She winks lightheartedly, her big hazel eyes filled with mischief.

"What's his name?" I quip, watching her cheeks pink and I realize there's a guy involved. Whenever she has a little plan formulating in that intelligent brain of hers she gets this look and I know I'm going to be involved somehow.

"What makes you think it's got anything to do with a guy?" She pops her hip, pinning me with a playful glare. Sipping my coffee, I savor the taste before answering her.

"Dakota, there's something all sparkly in those caramel gems and I'm not stupid. What is his name?" Rolling her eyes, she let's a giggle fall from her pouty lips.

"Well…" She drags the word out slowly and I know something's about to shock me. "It's just, you sort of know him." She snickers before drinking her own milky coffee. Narrowing my eyes, I watch another deep crimson blush appear on her cheeks.

"Mmhmm, I knew it. And who is this man I *sort of*

know?" I tip my head to the side in question.

"Axel,"—she sighs dramatically—"Sky, he's a God. That body, that accent, those lips that I want on every inch of my skin, and a smirk that makes me want to drop my panties instantly. I've been crushing for a little while now and…well… I want to make a move, but I don't want to go up to him, I want to play the naughty kitten. I'm going to drive him crazy because the way those blue orbs were piercing me from across the room last night, I know he wants to devour me." Her lips purse playfully as she reminisces about the man who I consider a friend.

I can't help laughing at the sweet, faraway look in her eyes. She's smitten. "You just need to speak to him," I respond nonchalantly. She snaps her gaze to mine and shakes her head. "Why not?"

"He's someone who likes the chase, he's said so himself, so I need you to teach me a routine that will make him lose it completely." She gives me the puppy dog eyes, because she knows I can't deny her anything when she does, and I nod. "Yay! Thank you, Phoenix." A quick peck on the cheek and she's racing into her bedroom. Shaking my head, I finish my coffee and rise from the stool.

"This is going to be a long day, isn't it?" I call to her and I hear her laugh.

"Yes, but you love me, so you don't mind." I stop at her bedroom door as she pulls on a pair of shorts. She's got a dancer's body, lithe, toned, and so sexy.

"I do love you, unfortunately." I giggle as she chucks a pillow at me. "I'll get ready and we'll go in about ten?"

"Perfect."

"Dakota, Skyla." We both turn to regard Theia as she nears us. We've just arrived for work and the place is dead quiet as I take a look around. "I've got something for you two." Her small grin tells me she has a booking, something naughty.

"And let me guess, it involves, me, Dakota, and a video camera?" I quip. We've been requested to play in the Eagle Room a few times because of the video recording option. Some poor asshole is going to take the video home and jerk himself off to us. Sad, but true.

"Indeed, I have two men, they've asked to watch you ladies play. There will be no contact with either of them," she explains, and I'm intrigued.

"Sounds interesting, we'll get changed." She nods in her efficient way, allowing Dakota and I to pass by as we head toward the dressing rooms.

"You've got an hour and they'll be here," she informs us, before we're out of earshot.

"I'm wearing my black and pink lingerie set," my little kitten tells me in excitement. Kota loves to be watched getting fucked, but the woman is naughty as hell and there's no one else I'd do this with. I don't know how Axe will handle it if they ever got together, he's not one for sharing.

As we step into the quiet of the dressing room, I sashay

over to my closet, pulling out the outfit I know will be perfect. An off-white silk pair of panties with tiny bows on each corner holding it against my hips. The matching bra is soft against my skin with a diamanté pendant, which clips between my breasts.

Once I'm changed, I settle on the stool at the dresser and turn on my hot iron. A few curls to frame my face with a light dusting of make-up gives me an innocent look. If only they knew the she-devil is about to blow their fucking minds.

"You're a picture of innocence this evening, Sky," Dakota comments, as she slides onto the stool beside me. Her black and pink corset hugs her curves and pushes her breasts up affording me a view of incredible cleavage.

"I figured since you're going for the dark, I'll go for the light. Give them a show for their money." I shrug as I twirl locks of hair in the iron, giving me springy curls.

"Ready?" she smiles as she rises to full height. I glance up to find Dakota poised and ready to go. Nodding, I slip on my heels and stand. We're almost the same height.

As we head into the main area of the club, I notice it's gotten busier since we arrived, and the crowd is gathered at the bar waiting on Heather to walk onto the stage.

As we head down the hallway, nerves kick in and a flutter in my belly has me wondering if I should have had a shot of Patron before walking in there. The silver door knob glistens, beckoning us closer. Dakota twists it and the door swings open easily. The scent of male cologne hits me immediately and as soon as we step inside we're greeted by the clients.

Both look to be in their early forties, one with a bit of dark scruff and the other clean shaven. Handsome and dressed in dark slacks with shiny loafers, their pristine white shirts look like they've just been dry cleaned. "Ladies," one of them murmurs, in a deep, seductive drawl, "you're quite the spectacle on stage, however we'd like to see what you can do in private."

"There's indeed a long list of things we could do in the privacy of this room." I challenge. "I understand you'd like to record the session?" I question, following Dakota further into the deep red room. He nods, regarding me with caramel colored eyes and a sinful smirk.

"Come here, Red," he commands, lowering his tone until it comes out almost gravelly. I stroll over to the sofa where they're both sitting. "I want you to turn, very slowly. I'd like to look at you," the strange request has my brows knitting together, but I obey, catching Dakota's confused gaze as I turn back toward them. "Beautiful."

"The little brunette, come here," the man on my right growls, and Dakota hurries toward him. "Are you going to show daddy the back of those pretty panties?" My heart rate spikes as I watch my little kitten turn her back to the man.

"Henry, it seems you've got a pert little one there, just like her cohort, Red, over here." He sits back, lifting a tumbler to his lips and my gaze follows his hand. "Sit in that chair." He points to the one they've conveniently positioned at the camera. Without argument, I stalk over to the seat in question and settle on the soft suede.

"Good girl,"—Henry smirks—"now open those slender legs, let's see what you have hidden between those toned thighs." With an unhurried pace, I spread my legs, keeping my eyes on the caramel gaze burning with lust and hunger. "Take one finger and stroke yourself over those angelic panties." Lifting the side of my mouth into a sultry smirk, I obey feeling the tender touch of my index finger. "Lou, doesn't that just look incredible," he tells his friend, with a chuckle that's thick with desire.

"Poppet, why don't you go join your friend. I want to see you strip her of those virtuous scraps of material, then you'll get naked for us too and kneel between her legs." He orders in a gruff tone. Dakota makes her way to me quickly, leaning in, she unhooks my bra, and then helps me out of my panties. I now sit bare in front of two men and my best friend.

Once Dakota's naked, she kneels between my legs, her big golden brown eyes peering up at me with mischief. "Now eat her bare cunt." The order is raspy, filled with hunger and I'm not sure who it comes from, but Kota doesn't disappoint. The camera is pointed right at us, capturing my best friend devouring my pussy like it's her favorite treat.

My head drops back as the sensation of her tongue lapping at my sex sends me into orbit, her fingers tease and stroke me while she sucks on my clit. My body bows off the chair and my hips buck toward her, needing more, wanting more.

"That's it, make her come on your tongue." The command comes from somewhere in the room. I'm so lost in the swirl of fingers inside me, and the pressure being placed on my clit and G spot, that all I can do is grip the arms of the chair and dig my nails in as I fly apart for the audience. "Now that was a show worth the money. Red, how about you show Poppet how much you appreciated her licking your sweet, little pussy." Snapping my gaze to him again, I watch him take a long sip of the amber liquid.

I shift slowly, my legs still trembling, but I manage to drop to my knees, allowing Dakota to sit, but before she can, a baritone interrupts us. "Kneel, Poppet, we want to see Red eat that sexy little ass while she devours your cunt." My Kitten quickly kneels on the chair with a grip on the back. She glances at me and we both wink.

Hooking my fingers in the waistband of her panties, I tug them over her supple ass and down her smooth, tanned thighs. I lift one hand and swat one cheek then the other. Her squeals of delight echo around us and I can't help smiling. I grasp her ass and lean in, slowly licking from her hardened little bud all the way to her puckered entrance.

"Christ, now that's a vision. You two are the perfect match, incredible." Ignoring our audience, I lap at Dakota's sweet, pussy. Her body shudders, but I don't stop. Her moans and whimpers tell me she's unravelling and I bask in the fact that I know her as well as she knows me. I land another swat on her ass while plunging two fingers inside her body.

"Sky!" she cries out, and I know she's close, I can feel her pulsing. "Please!" Another shout and I tease a finger into her ass. Her body locks and she screams as she shatters before me.

Moments pass and I watch her slowly come back down from the high. Before we even register what's happened, the two men stalk toward us smiling. "You two are beautiful, thank you," Henry offers quietly, it's when Lou smiles and leans in that my breathing halts.

"Skyla and Kota, filthy little angels, perfect." And with that, we're left alone.

"Well, that was…" My words taper off, wondering what the fuck just happened.

"Fucking hot!" Dakota giggles and I can't help chuckling myself.

Kael

Two paintings.

Finished.

Sitting back, I look at each of them. I never thought I'd manage this. It's been almost forty-eight hours. I haven't slept, my mind kept replaying every part of her, of us. Past and present.

As soon as I close my eyes, she's there. A force of nature, something I can't bring myself to live without. When I left her all I had was a photograph. Now, I have her in the flesh. Tonight I'll be inside her again. Rising to my feet, I pull off my T-shirt, and head into my bathroom. Shoving off the jeans I wear while painting, I turn on the shower and wait for it to heat.

The steam billows around me and in the fog, I glance

at my reflection. My dark eyes are bloodshot from not sleeping, but it was worth every moment. Stepping into the shower, I revel in the warmth of the spray.

I close my eyes, picturing my girl, my woman, because that's what she is. Mine. Her body twirling on that pole is enough to have me hard, throbbing, and aching for her. As the water cascades down my shoulders all I want is to once again have her in my arms, in my bed.

Back in the bedroom, I find a pair of faded blue jeans and a black T-shirt. I'm going to find her and take her out. On a real date. The thought alone has me rushing through the apartment like a teenager with a crush on the prettiest girl in school.

Memories of our past are the only thing that got me through the lonely nights, but it's time to make new ones. I need to find a way to tell her the truth, but not before I'm sure she's not going to tell me to go to hell.

With one last look at my appearance, I head into the living room and grab my keys and phone. It's just hit midday and the heat is already unbearable as I slip into the driver's seat of my Jeep. The streets are busy as I head toward Inferno.

This is the second time I'm going to walk in there, and I wish it could be my last, but I know it won't be that easy to get her out of there. I'd love to throw her over my shoulder like a caveman and drag her back to my apartment. Never letting her leave.

The parking lot is mostly empty when I pull up to the club with only six other cars. Parking near the door, I exit the vehicle and make my way towards the entrance. When I push the door, it slides inward with ease, allowing me access to the dimly lit, cavernous space.

The pretty dark-haired hostess, who I've known all my life, glances up and offers me a smile. "Kael, it's good to see you here. It's been way too long, brother." She rounds the desk to give me a hug and I instantly calm, knowing she'll help me. "How can I help you?" She steps back and gives me her full attention.

"I'd like to see Skyla." I tell her hastily, hoping she doesn't turn me away.

"Well, she's busy training at the moment—" she responds, but I cut her off because there's no way I'm leaving until I see my Phoenix.

"Theia..."

"I know, Kael." She smiles, amusement dancing in her eyes.

"You didn't tell me she's here," I meet her warm gaze. "I'm not leaving here until I see her, so if you'd like to tell me where I can wait, I'll happily do so, and pay for the time."

Her mouth lifts into a smirk as she regards me through narrowed eyes. "Well then, since you're so adamant to see the fiery vixen, I'll escort you to a table where you'll be able to watch and not disturb them."

"Them?"

She nods excitedly as she watches my reaction. "Yes, she and the little kitten, Kota, are playing on stage." She gestures toward the pole dancing stage and I take in the two beauties dressed in skimpy shorts and tank tops. "Follow me." My sister escorts me to a small round table in the corner away from prying eyes where I settle into a chair.

"Thank you," I murmur, and she leaves me, heading back to her desk. I lean back, relaxing with my eyes trained on the two women as I enjoy the show. The little brunette with the pert ass has her legs wrapped around the pole, twirling like a ballerina.

She stops suddenly, and drops to her feet when Skyla directs, "No, take this hand and lower it." Dakota steps away from the metal pole and allows the fiery redhead to show her. Her lithe body spins, her legs spread and I'm awarded a view like no other. The tiny pair of black Lycra shorts hide the bare little cunt I know is hidden there, but the way her toned legs move is enough to have me straining in my jeans.

"Quite the sight aren't they?" I glance at the man joining me. I saw him the other night, and I know he works with Axe, but the way he's salivating over the two beauties has my hackles rising.

"They are." I drag my gaze from him and give my full attention to the stage.

The music changes and "Bunny Park" by Cnsrd starts. The two naughty girls start swaying, giggling, and shock the shit out of me when they kiss. Not your average friendly one, but a slow sensual one. It's as if they're lost to the music.

"Which one are you waiting for? Or are you wanting

them both?" he asks, stealing my attention.

"The redhead," I respond easily, my eyes never leaving the stage. As if she feels me looking, her gaze darts up and her eyes lock on mine sending heat sizzling through me. The side of her mouth lifts slightly, a smile, small and intimate meant only for me. I watch her lean in and whisper into Dakota's ear, the little brunette nods and glances at me with a knowing smile.

Skyla makes her way off the stage and toward me. The sight of her long, slender legs, those curves and the way her tits bounce have me groaning. "I'll leave you to it man, lucky fucker." The man beside me chuckles, but the only thing I am focused on is the firebird nearing me.

"You're here…" Her voice tapers off as she regards me with those emerald pools.

"I am." Pushing up, I gesture for her to sit, but she shakes her head.

She crosses her arms in front of her and I can't help my gaze straying for a moment to her cleavage that taunts me from the tight confines of her tank top. Tipping her head to the side, she questions quietly, "Why?"

"Do you normally question your regular clients?" Ignoring her question, I offer one of my own. Fire blazes in her eyes and her cheeks darken with a blush.

"No, I just… Well, I didn't think I'd see you again. Did you book a room?" Her gaze flits between me, the table, then she settles her gaze on the floor. I can tell she's nervous.

"I've actually come to book you,"—her gaze snaps to

me and I continue—"for the day. I want to take you out for lunch." I reach for her hand, but she doesn't allow me the pleasure of accepting the gesture.

"I can't. I don't… I mean, this isn't what I do." She fumbles for an excuse, but I'm not taking no for an answer. Reaching for her arm, I settle my hand on her shoulder and stroke the smooth skin with my thumb.

"I'd pay for your time, please?" I meet her gaze dead on, wanting her to fight me because she's so fucking hot when she does. A quick shrug and she glances back at the stage where her friend is swapping with another girl with long blonde hair.

"I need to talk to Dakota first," she murmurs, before meeting my eyes.

"I'll wait right here." I release her, settling myself on the chair.

She turns to walk away and the way her hips sway in those tiny shorts has me once again hardening in my jeans. Her ass is pert, round, and there are so many filthy things I want to do to it. To mark it with my hand print.

Jesus the things I want to do to you, little firebird. So many fucking delicious ways I can and will enjoy you. Soon, Phoenix. Real fucking soon.

Skyla

"Dakota," I call to her, as I near the side of the stage where she's shrugging on her jumper. She turns to regard me with that knowing smile.

"Who's the hottie?" She questions quietly.

"It's the client who was here two nights ago. He wants to take me to lunch, I don't—"

"Oh. My. God. You have to go!" Her hands reach up to grip my shoulders and she shakes me back and forth a few times like she's trying to shake some sense into me.

"Do you think?"

"Yes, my God, Red. You can't deny that man. Have you seen him?" She gawks at me like I'm stupid, perhaps I am. He is gorgeous. Devastatingly so. I'm just concerned I'll let my heart get the better of me and then I'll end up hurt and alone.

"I have, that's the problem, babe. He scares me," I admit quietly, feeling a tug in my chest. She's the only person in my life I'll admit this to. We're like sisters, and I wouldn't trust anyone with my feelings more than I do her.

"Babe, look at me," she implores, and I do, "if he came back here after one night with you just to take you to lunch, surely that must mean something?" My voice of reason. That's what she is. Yes, she's right. I cast a quick glance behind me and find him watching us intently. "I'm not saying he's going to propose, but he's waiting on you and I don't think he'd like it very much if you don't get your sexy, little ass, that he's been staring at all this time, over there. Have fun, babe. Be happy, you need to let the past go." Once again her words hit me right in the chest.

I do need to let go of the agony from my past. "Fine," I say, rolling my eyes as she squeals in delight. "I'll see you later." I pull her into my arms and plant a soft kiss on her cheek. "Love you, Koty."

"Love you too, Red."

Dakota flops onto one of the chairs as I grab my jean shorts and pull them over my small Lycra boy shorts I train in. At least I don't have to go backstage to change. The flowing T-shirt I've brought along falls easily over my tank top. "Are you leaving those on?" She points at my shoes and I nod. They're not too high, and they work with my outfit.

"Yeah, do you think they're too much?"

Her lips purse into a pout as she drags those mischievous eyes, from my toes up to my head. "You look gorgeous as always, go knock him dead." She winks playfully, but before I turn to leave, she leans forward and murmurs, "And I bet he's dying to fuck you in those." A giggle falls from her lips and I feel myself blush. Jesus, she can be naughty.

"Shh! I'll see you later." Turning, I make my way back to the man who's sitting there like a God. Beautiful, majestic, and downright sinful.

"Since I'm not working, you don't have to pay for my time." I smile, and his face cracks into a heart stopping grin. As we make our way past one of the girls, Brie, at the front desk, her eyes widen and she grins, giving me a wink. My cheeks heat with a blush.

"I would have been happy to, you know," he murmurs in my ear, and an elicit shudder wracks my body.

"I'm sure you would," I joke playfully as we exit the club. The sun is bright and I'm glad I've dressed for the weather.

"Over here, gorgeous." Kael places a hand on my lower back and electricity zips through me. We reach a Jeep which is a deep crimson, so dark it's almost black. He leans in to open the door and his scent swirls around me like an intoxicating cloud. As I slip into the seat, I don't miss the hungry stare he roams my legs with and I have to bite the inside of my cheek to keep from grinning like an idiot.

I watch him round the car and hop into the driver's

seat.

Before he starts the engine, I question, "So where exactly are we going?"

"Well, here's the thing. Before you refuse, I want you to hear me out"—he cuts a quick peek my way, and I nod—"I'd like you to pose for me," he lets out in a rush.

"What?"

He starts the engine and pulls out onto the road, while cutting short glimpses at me as he responds. "I'm an artist, and I'd like you to pose for me. I'm busy with some stills for a photography series and I'd like you as my muse," he says quietly, and my gaze darts to him in question.

Me?

"I don't know," I whisper my unconvincing response, but I know he heard it. I direct my eyes back out the window to watch the city pass us by. I feel my nerves settle as he slows and pulls into a diner not far from the club.

The one he's chosen for lunch is one of my favorite places. Dakota and I come here all the time, they make the best burgers in town. When he doesn't get out immediately, I turn to regard him again. There's so much excitement dancing in his eyes I don't want to say no. But for me to be a muse? I don't know.

He offers me a small smile and hope beckons. What can I do? I'm helpless around him. All I want to do is climb into his lap and ask him to let me be anything he wants. *Even a pet?* Shaking my head, I let out a sigh and I meet his gaze.

Kael

I can see the doubt in her eyes. Her emotions were always written on her face, that's how I learned how to read her so well. I want to tell her who I am, to come out with it and finally move forward, but before I do, I want to make sure she's not going to run.

"I'm not about to steal you away and tie you up in my dungeon,"—the words flicker memories for us both— "actually, I will tie you up, but when I do, you'll love it," I chuckle, trying to inject some humor into the air around us which is so heavy with her uncertainty.

"Let me think about it over lunch." She smiles and her eyes light up with amusement. I know she's not used to being alone with someone, especially not a man who actually cares for her, fuck if I'm honest, a man who loves her.

"Okay, let's get you fed, beautiful." I wink before exiting the car. Rounding the front, I open her door and offer my hand, which she gratefully accepts. She easily falls into step beside me and I can't help but feel as if we've finally been given a chance to be a normal couple.

Yes, I've been with other women before, but never dated. I've never had the inclination to want more, so I spent the five years we'd been apart burying myself in women who meant nothing to me.

We find a booth and a waitress strolls over with a big smile. "Hi honey." She beams at my girl.

"Hey, it's good to see you again." Skyla offers a smile that makes my heart stutter. The one I want on her face permanently.

"It is. We've got a few new specials today which include the double cheeseburger with fries," she responds, glancing between us, "so, what can I get you both?"

"I'll have a coffee and get me one of those cheeseburgers and fries, extra fries and Skyla over here will have the same." I sit back, relaxing in the soft faux red pleather bench seat.

The little firebird gawks at me, but doesn't say anything before handing the menu to the waitress. Once we're alone, her gaze bores into me. "I am capable of ordering my own food, Kael." My name falls from her lips and my cock thickens in my jeans, thankfully hidden by the table. I clear my throat, trying to hide the growl that rumbles in my chest.

"I know, but I figured you'd want the burger, I could tell how your eyes lit up when she mentioned it." I offer a wink and she blushes a beautiful shade of pink which in turn has me wanting to see that same hue on her pert little ass.

"I'll give you points for that," she quips playfully, "so, tell me, how would you like me to pose for you, if I decide to."

"I want you in those heels." I gesture to the shoes she's currently wearing. They're shimmery black pumps that put at least four inches on her height. "Perhaps a little thong as well, but I want to capture you. Your body, those curves and those incredible tits," I tell her honestly. Something akin to desire flits across her face and I know she's turned on when a soft blush darkens her cheeks. She squirms, but it's such a slight movement, if I didn't know how to read this woman, I would have missed it.

"And what happens after?" she murmurs, but before I can tell her I'm going to fuck her senseless, the waitress returns with our coffees.

As soon as she's out of earshot, I lean in and see those emeralds darken. "I'm going to rip off the panties, and I'm going to make you come on my tongue, my fingers, and then I'll make you scream until your throat is hoarse, as I fuck you with my cock."

A gasp falls from her lips, but she meets my stare, challenging me. "You're overly confident there, Kael, but I'll take you up on that offer because I'd like to see you *rise* to the occasion." She dips her finger in the coffee and swirls it around, then brings it to her mouth, sucking it between her lips and if I wasn't hard before, I sure as fuck am now.

"Oh, Phoenix, I'll rise and I'll make sure you're soaring with me."

Just then, our food arrives and I watch her dig in. Even though we're sitting in a diner, and it's one of the most casual places in the city, she still looks as if she's sitting in a five-star restaurant.

Elegant, beautiful, delicate.

Halfway through her burger, she lifts her gaze and meets mine. "What?" she quizzes, and I chuckle at the ketchup on the side of her mouth. Reaching over, I swipe it with my thumb and bring it to my mouth.

"You're beautiful," I offer, and dig into my own meal.

The rest of lunch is silent and every now and then, I glance up at her, taking in the beauty that's ensnared me once again.

As soon as I've paid the bill, we head back to the jeep. I open her door and watch her slide into the seat. It's hypnotic how her body moves with such precision. Her slender legs are lightly tanned giving her a bronze glow and I can't wait to have those thighs wrapped around my head, then my waist. "Are you going to stare at me all day?" she quips playfully, and I realize I'd been drooling over her.

Before shutting the door, I lean in and question, "yes, tell me you'll pose for me?" With my forearm on the roof of the car and my eyes trained on her, I wait for her response.

I need to know. A sly smirk plays on her perfect lips and she nods. Releasing a breath, I didn't know I was holding, I shut the door and make my way to the driver's side.

The drive to my apartment is filled with an intensity that steals my breath and when I park the car, I turn to her. "You don't have to do this."

"I want to,"—she grins—"or are you worried you'll not live up to your earlier promise?"

Chuckling, I shake my head, "Don't you concern your pretty little head, I'll make good on my words." I get out of the car and before I can open her door, she's out, standing in my driveway looking like a vision. I guide her to the front door and unlock it, allowing her to enter my apartment for the first time.

The clicking lock echoes in my ears. Realizing I have her alone, in my home, my nerves kick in. I feel like a teenager with his first girlfriend while his parent's are away.

"So, where do you want me?" She pivots on those fuck me heels and the look she gives me has my jeans tightening and my mind filling with filthy images of just how and where I want her. Bound and helpless, writhing under me, whimpering and pleading as I devour every inch of her.

"You're welcome to change in the bathroom, but the chaise over there will be perfect. I'll get the toys," I murmur, and her eyes widen.

"Toys?" she quips.

"The cuffs, darling, I told you I'm tying you up."

Before she can respond, I make my way into the bedroom and retrieve the thick leather cuffs.

In the living room I find her draped on the gray suede chaise. I drag my gaze from those heels, slowly up her long, lithe legs, to the tiny thong that barely covers her pussy and up to her firm, full tits. When I finally meet her gaze, I lift my mouth into a knowing smirk. "You like the view?" she questions.

"Fuck yes." The words are a deep growl and it takes all my restraint not to fuck her right now. I stalk over and make quick work of binding her wrists and positioning her on all fours with her arms draped over the back of the deep blue suede chaise longue. Her pert ass sticks out and her curves are every bit as inviting as they were all those years ago.

I grab my camera, and snap a few shots, directing her as I do and she obeys, silently and without complaint. Her poses are elegant, yet sexy. Dirty, yet playful. And I find myself licking my lips hungrily as I crave to take her. When she moves it's almost cat-like, her legs splay for one shot and I find myself focused on the apex of her thighs. Needing to bury myself inside her.

After two rolls of film, I near her and she watches me like a little kitten, ready to swat at a toy. Lifting my hand, I trail my fingertips from her feet, up those limbs that I want to plant kisses on, just missing her pussy, I then tease her hip and the curve of her breast. "So beautiful." My tone is reverent. She deserves it all and I vow to give it to her.

"Kael." My name is a whimper, a soft, seductive moan

and I'm ready to take her. She peers up at me under those thick eyelashes and I nod. Cementing my stance, I watch her lift bound hands and undo my jeans.

"Stand for me." I step back, pulling off my T-shirt, and watch her rise dressed in the tiniest little thong. Without a word, I drop to my knees before her and an audible gasp has me peering up at her. She's always been the one to kneel and I want her to feel the power in having me at her feet.

I reach up, hooking my fingers in the waistband of her panties, and before I tug them down, I run my nose up her inner thighs, reveling in the scent of my woman.

I pull down so slowly, I can see her body tremble. The material slips down the curve of her ass, once her pussy is bared to me, I let out a growl, animalistic and primal.

Mine.

"You smell so fucking good, I'm going to feast on you all day."

"Jesus, Kael, stop teasing me," she whimpers, and I can't help chuckling. I plant a soft kiss on her mound, the smooth lips feel warm against my mouth.

I rise up and undo the cuffs, my eyes locked on hers.

"Do you trust me?" I ask, quietly waiting for her. Expecting her to refuse, she shocks me by nodding slowly. "Good girl," I murmur.

Stepping back, I leave her for a moment to grab the onyx silk rope and when I turn to her, those emerald eyes peer at me with inquisitive concentration.

"Arms behind your back," I order, and she obeys

beautifully. My sweet little pet. I weave an intricate pattern binding both arms together. In turn, her breasts jut out and her nipples harden. Leaning in, I whisper in her ear, "Does this turn you on, Phoenix?" The nickname sends a tremble through her.

"Yes, Sir." Her raspy tone is evidence that she's being truthful and I nod. When I left her we hadn't done any of this and I wonder about her past.

Slowly, I finish up the knot at her wrists, then trail my fingers down to her thighs and leisurely up to the pert cheeks of her ass. I grip them, squeezing them, earning me a soft mewl. My cock throbs painfully and I place a hand on her hip. "Bend for me, baby." Her body folds and I spread her legs. "Trust me, Pai—Skyla." My slip up goes unnoticed when I stroke the drenched spot between her thighs. "You're so perfect," I murmur against the sensitive smooth flesh and her knees buckle.

"Kael, I can't—"

"You can, baby, just breathe." Once again, I grip her beautiful, creamy ass and open her to my gaze. Inhaling her sweet scent, I flick my tongue out, lapping at her pussy.

"Oh, my God!" she cries out, only heightening my need for her. I lick her from that hardened, little bud, all the way to her tight, puckered entrance I'm dying to plunge into. Again and again, I repeat the action. My tongue dives into her tight cunt and she flies apart, soaring like the firebird I know she is.

Her legs tremble as I rise and lick my lips, savoring her honeyed release. "Up," I command, and she straightens.

I spin her around and meet her glazed stare. "Did I make good on my first promise?" I quip, her body still shuddering in my arms.

"Yes, you did." Her lips lift into a smile. I tug on the knot allowing the rope to fall free from her arms.

"Now for part two." I wink, leaning in, I lift her in my arms and walk her to the sofa. Before I sit back, I shove my jeans and boxers down. With a tight grip on her hips, I tug her over me. "Sit on my dick, firebird." She straddles me, and I position my throbbing erection at her tight heat.

Her head falls back as she sinks down on my length, her body taking me inch by rock hard inch. "Fuck, Kael," she mewls, and then whimpers.

"Christ, ride me. Take your pleasure, I want to watch you come for me." I sit back, watching her tits bounce as her hips undulate. She grips my shoulders and her nails dig into the muscle. Her pace is slow at first, but when I reach for her clit and circle it with my thumb she hastens her movements and I feel her pulse and quiver around me.

Our bodies move in sync, my hips lift, meeting hers. I drive deep into her, claiming her like I should have done all those years ago. I want to tell her, in this moment, but I chicken out again. Reaching up, I tweak her nipples, tugging them hard until she screams my name as her release wracks her body. Seconds later, I grunt through mine, filling her. Marking her as mine.

Skyla

Sunlight bathes my bedroom in a warm glow as I crack my eyelids. After my initial date with Kael, we've been texting back and forth. He had to leave on a business trip and even though it hasn't been very long, we've grown close through messages and late night phone calls.

It's been almost a month and memories of that day have replayed in my mind on a loop. That gentle touch was too much for my heart to bear. I'm so used to men being rough, that a tender stroke or a feather-light kiss sets me on edge.

My phone vibrates and I know it's him. Even though he's busy he'll message me every day. Slowly this man is breaking down my walls, brick by brick.

Firebird, I'm missing you. I'll be back soon. I hope you've saved a dance for me. x

Smiling at the words, I hit reply and promise him a dance when he's back.

Pushing off the bed, I pull on a pair of sweats and a T-shirt. Lacing up my sneakers, I pull my hair into a tight ponytail and head into the kitchen, but before I get to my destination, I smack into Dakota. "Shit, sorry." I pull the earphones from my ears and meet her inquisitive gaze.

"Where are you going, Red?" she questions, using one of the few nicknames she's become accustomed to calling me.

"Out. I need air." Trying not to meet her non-believing stare is difficult because she can read me like a book, open or closed, and I know no matter how hard I try, she'll drag the reason for my dismissiveness from me.

"Don't bullshit me, babe. Tell me." She reaches for my hand and pulls me into her bedroom. "What happened?"

"Kael"—I flop onto the bed beside her—"he's away and we've chatted on the phone, but... I'm fucked, Dakota..." My words taper off, and when I lift my watery gaze, I find her staring at me.

"You're falling for him," she whispers, and I nod feeling the tears burn my eyes. "Oh, my sweet little Red. Come here." She pulls me into a warm hug and I feel the calm she always brings me. "He must feel something if he's still in contact with you," she reassures, and I nod silently.

The fear of falling in love with someone has always been there, at the back of my mind taunting me. Now that it's happening, I wonder if I'll be able to give my heart to him fully when I'm still in love with someone else.

We don't talk for a long while and I know she's waiting for me to say something. "I need fresh air. I'll see you later, okay?" I murmur, and she releases me. Nodding, she allows me to rise and walk to the entrance of her bedroom.

"Don't be late. We've got a Sapphire booking today," she calls, before I exit and I nod without looking back. Right now, I need to clear my mind.

Once my earbuds are in and my running playlist is on, I hit the street. The early morning air is humid as I make my way down the road. My legs cry out from the strain, but I push past the ache.

As I slow down, I take in my surroundings and realize it will take me another twenty minutes to get back. There are always tourists walking around photographing everything they can. I pass a few couples strolling happily hand in hand and I wonder briefly if I'll ever have that.

You're just a toy. Filthy and disgusting. Only good for men to use.

Those words linger. They seep into my very being, leaving me hollow.

"Fancy meeting you here." A familiar baritone has me spinning around. Kael. He's dressed in faded, ripped jeans with paint splattered across them. His white T-shirt is ruined with various shades of color, but he looks incredible. No other man has ever made me ache with a mere glance, but with him, those cocoa-colored eyes render me speechless.

I want to run up to him, but I don't. "You said you were getting back soon, not that you're back already," I respond, and it comes out more accusing that I meant it to. His eyes narrow, and his quizzical expression makes me aware that he's noticed the accusation in my words.

Dark pools stare at me and I can't help clenching my thighs. They're sexy—alluring even—and I want to spend more time with him to delve into this man.

"I did say soon, you're right, but I wanted to surprise you. Let's have coffee?" He cocks his head to the side. There's hope flitting across his face, and I find myself nodding. I shouldn't do this. The voice inside my head is screaming, but I ignore her and walk toward him.

"You were gone for a long time," I state quietly, feeling foolish as soon as the words have left my lips. I don't want him to think I've been missing him, or even thinking about him. Yes, we had a date or two, but that didn't mean anything.

"Phoenix, you know I had work to do. The client who commissioned those paintings asked me to fly to Chicago and I couldn't refuse. They have a gallery booked for an exhibition and I had to scope it out," he says, reaching a hand for me.

"Oh." Feeling silly for saying something, I peer up at him.

"Did you miss me?" he quips. The all-knowing smirk lifts one side of his mouth, and I bite the inside of my cheek to keep from smiling.

"No, of course not."

"Okay, Phoenix," he murmurs, placating me. "Come on?"

When he reaches for me again, I slip my hand in his and nod. "Fine." We fall into step beside each other and walk in silence. I keep my breaths even, but my heart is racing. "So you really are a full time artist?" I trail my eyes over him, taking in the shabby appearance.

"Yes, the contract has been approved so it seems like I'll be calling Chicago home in the near future," he tells me proudly.

He's leaving.

My heart plummets and I nod, glancing up at him. His scruff is longer than I normally like on a man, but on him, I'd take it. His long hair is curly and falls just past his shoulders. He's definitely beautiful.

"Chicago? Wow, congratulations. That's... that's good." I stumble over my words, but he doesn't notice as he stops outside an intimate coffee shop. He opens the door, allowing me to enter first, and I'm assaulted by the smell of roasted coffee and the scent of freshly baked treats, which have my stomach grumbling.

"Let's get some drinks and I'll tell you more about it." He ushers me to the counter with his fingertips at the base of my spine, which once again send heated tingles through me. The memory of his hands on my body is still fresh on my mind. "Coffee, babe?"

"Yes, please." I smile while glancing around the room.

While he orders, I find us a small booth in the corner. I slip in and wait for him, thinking about how a man who works with his hands is the ultimate fantasy.

When he sets the cup in front of me, I lift it to my lips, taking a tentative sip and enjoying the flavor. Our gazes lock and his searing stare immediately falls to my wet lips.

"You're good at that." He gestures to my mouth as he takes a sip of his own drink. Shrugging, I glance around feeling embarrassed. We met as client and dancer in a nightclub, he's paid to fuck me, yet here we are, sitting in a coffee shop like a normal couple. "I want to learn who you are, Phoenix," he states with curiosity, staring at me a little too intently. His eyes bore into me and I shift uncomfortably under the scrutiny.

"I'm Sky. You know that. Dancer at Inferno." My response is short, cold, and I can tell it annoys him from the scowl on his face. He takes another gulp of his coffee, but doesn't shift his gaze from me. My eyes settle on his Adam's apple and I watch it work as he swallows.

"You know what I meant," he utters in frustration.

Meeting his brown eyes, I respond, wanting to change the subject. "So, are you going to tell me about this contract you've got?"

I don't miss the quick narrowing of his eyes. "Don't fucking do that." His voice lowers into a growl, and I'm fucked because it's got my pussy aching for another feel of his thick cock.

The growl, the tone, everything, it's too fucking much. It's as if the man who left me in that hell is sitting before me, and I can't take that pain again. It took me years to get over him. I'm still a wreck whenever I think about him.

As much as I thought it could be him, I'm not stupid enough to think my life could possibly work out. Kael is leaving and when he goes I'll be alone again. The thought has my heart squeezing, leaving me utterly breathless. I'm not putting myself through heartbreak again. "This is done," I retort, meeting his glare and swallowing down the last of my drink before I push out of the seat. "Thanks for the coffee."

He doesn't come after me, and I don't expect him to. As soon as I step out of the store, I turn left and make my way back down the road.

I'm not very far when I hear him. "I'm not done with you." His shout sends a shiver of lust through me. *I'm done with you.* "Sky, please." I hear him say.

Please. A word no man has ever said to me. Except the one person I put all my trust in, only to have it ripped away. I thought he was my angel, but instead he turned out to be a liar.

Spinning on my heel, I face him. There's so much emotion in his gaze, it scares me to death. "What? You want another go? Well, you know where I work. I don't spread my legs for free," I hiss, as anger slowly seeps into my heart.

He just stares at me for a moment, the sounds of the bustling street filling the space between us. "So you'd rather shake your half naked ass on a stage for vile men to throw money at, than date me, is that it?" His question cuts me so deep that I have to school my expression in order to not gape at him. We're a few feet apart, and I want to run up to him and ask him—no, beg him—to save me. Tell him that I want nothing more than just that. But I don't. I can't let myself feel hope. Not one ounce.

"Yes," I say instead, with conviction. And with that, I turn and walk away, leaving him staring at my retreating form. I can feel every inch of my skin ignite as those scorching coffee pools burn into me.

Since our argument on the sidewalk I haven't seen him in the club. Even though every day he calls and texts me—messages I've just deleted—I still think about him.

All. The. Fucking. Time.

I've known the man all of a few months and he's not left my mind since. I want him, I really fucking do, but he's leaving for a better life. When he told me he was heading to Chicago, I almost begged him to take me with him. But what would he want with a woman like me. Someone who can't give him anything more than a fuck.

Memories of where I've come from assault me at a rapid pace, stealing my breath when I remember my past. Taking in my reflection, I recall being in *that* place with such clarity it's as if I'm still there. When I wasn't given a choice but instead told what to do.

A trained toy.

Whenever it comes to mind, I remember *him*—the man who wore the mask, the one who made me feel—and it hurts. An ache, so deep in my chest, stifles me in ways I've never felt before, or since.

My naivety and innocence allowed him in, into my body and my heart.

The agony is still there.

I don't know if it will ever go away.

I loved and I lost.

And I promised myself never again.

That's why now that I'm wiser, I don't allow emotion to cloud my judgment. I'm only here to dance, and with the occasional client, fuck. No emotion.

Kael almost thawed me, melted the ice around my heart, but even he failed.

My face is shimmery and my eyes glow with the dark liner around them.

Perfect.

Pulling the black stockings up my thighs, I clip them onto my garter belt. The red and charcoal corset hugs my curves. The tiny matching thong cups my cunt like a glove. Snug fit.

In the hallway, I see the other girls heading toward the various booths and stages.

"Skyla." Theia strolls up to me in a black pencil skirt that stops just above her knee, and a beautiful silk blouse that hints at her deep rose-colored bra beneath. "I've got a gentleman who requested a private dance with you. Asked for you by name. I offered one of the other girls, but he was adamant." She smirks, her lips lift playfully and I'm staring at her shocked.

"Did he say why he wanted me specifically?" She shakes her head, no, and I continue, "Did you let boss man know I'm booked?"

A swift nod answers me, then she leans in with her lips at my ear and whispers conspiratorially, "Yeah, this guy has paid fifty grand for you." My heart thuds in my chest. Jesus Christ, that's a fucking bundle for a dance.

"Are you sure? Like, I mean…"

"No kidding, babe. Raven room, your favorite. Have fun." She winks and leaves me to wander to the long hallway where our VIP rooms are situated.

I've been doing this for so long, I should be used to it. Heading down the hallway to where I'm about to give some lucky bastard the dance of his life, my mind wonders what Kael would say if he were here.

When he asked if I'd rather do this than date him before I walked away, I said yes, but deep down I know it was a lie. There's nothing more I'd like than for him to walk in here and throw me over his shoulder.

It will never happen, I just need to come to terms with it, but the thought that I'll never have him hurts. After a few months, the pain will dull, and I'll be over it. But now that it's fresh in my mind, I can't help allowing it to overtake me.

If only I'd listened. Maybe if I'd given him a chance and not been so stubborn and dismissive. If only he'd not been so easy to push away. I can spend days with *what ifs* and *whys*, but ultimately, it was me. My choice. My decision. Yes, I'm an idiot. Now I've got to suck it up and live with it.

At the black door, I inhale a deep breath, push thoughts of Kael out of my mind, and twist the knob.

Kael

It's been too long.

Work kept me in Chicago or I would have come to see her sooner. After our argument, I was adamant to get back here and shake some sense into her. I would have barged my way in, thrown her over my shoulder and walked out of here. But I couldn't, and I know if I had even tried that she'd have shut down. So I've decided to go this route. I'll pay for now, but this will be the last fucking time I do. Because after today, she's mine. Only fucking mine.

I couldn't come back here and look into those beautiful eyes only to see the anger she had stored away for so long directed at me. Even though I deserved every ounce of it.

But today all bets are off. She's going to see me and she's going to fucking talk to me. My mind flits back while

I wait for her, remembering my sister's expression when I walked in.

"Brother?" She grins happily as I walk in. Rounding her desk, she pulls me into a hug so tight I have to fight for breath. I return the gesture, inhaling my sister's jasmine scented perfume. She hasn't changed. I've missed her so much, my heart hurts. It's taken me five years to walk in here when I knew she was just down the road. "What can I do for you?" she asks, when we step away from each other.

Meeting her blue gaze, I murmur, "I'm here for someone in particular." Leaning on the desk, I hope she can help me.

"Skyla?" she asks, without hesitation.

"Paige." Her name sounds wrong on my lips. My sister's eyes widen in shock and she regards me with curiosity. "Or yes, Skyla." I nod at her query. She's always known, all this time and she didn't tell me. As anger floods my mind, I push it back. I was the one who walked away.

"Yes, please. I want her in the Raven Room all night," I tell her with confidence. Recalling the menu I received when I came here with Axel the first time, I know this will cost an arm and a leg, but nothing will deter me from being with her again. Making her see that she's mine.

She nods. "That's an expensive option."

I hear the warning in her tone and I pull out my card. "This should cover it." I watch as she swipes it, hitting keys on the computer and then she rises, handing me back the plastic money.

"I'm happy to see you, Kael. She misses you, I can tell." My sister's confession sparks hope in my chest and I can't help *smiling. "Follow me." As we head farther into the club, she turns into the hallway that leads toward the bedrooms. Once we reach the right door, Theia hands me the key and my heart gallops in my chest, thudding painfully against my ribs as if it's about to break its way out.*

"Thank you, baby sister," I murmur, and she leans up on her tiptoes to plant a kiss on my cheek.

"Good luck," she offers, then turns and leaves me standing outside my future.

Shaking my head, I glance at the door as it swings open, and I'm met with the feisty redhead dressed in nothing more than the tiniest thong I have ever seen and a red and charcoal corset that pushes her full breasts up giving me an eyeful of her incredible cleavage. Her stockings are sheer and they're clipped to a garter which looks stunning on her curves.

"What are you doing here?" she questions harshly, but steps into the room and shuts the door behind her. I'm on my feet in seconds and close the distance between us.

"I've come to talk to you." I lower my voice in response.

She squares her shoulders and peers up at me.

"Talking is the same rate as fucking." She stalks past me, but I don't let her get that far. I grip her arm, tugging her against me so our bodies are flush, and I can feel the heat of her softly tanned skin. I grip both her hips, spin around and press her between me and the closed door.

Leaning in, I run my nose up the side of her neck,

inhaling the sweet scent of her. "Then we'll just have to talk while we're fucking, won't we, Phoenix?" Her gasp fans over my ear and I grin.

I reach for her throat and my other hand pushes between her legs. Her body trembles and my cock hardens. "Is this what you want? You want me to treat you like a whore? Because I will." A soft whimper falls from her beautiful mouth.

"Kael." My name on her lips is like fuel, dripping slowly onto the embers of my heart, sparking my desire. And I know she's going to burn me alive.

"Shh, you wanted me to pay to see you, so I'll bow to your wishes. But only this one time. You know why?" My fingers tease her smooth sex through the tiny thong. "Because I want you. I want this"—slipping my hand into her panties, I cup her cunt—"to be mine. Exclusively."

"I—"

Before she can respond, I drive two fingers into her— deep inside her body—owning her with my hand. Soon I'll be claiming her with my cock.

"This is what you were thinking about these past few months without me. Isn't it, baby?" I finger fuck her roughly, tightening my hold on her neck. "You thought about my cock while those assholes fucked you, didn't you? And before you fell asleep at night, you touched this pussy—my pussy—isn't that right?" My hand moves faster, and her gaze meets mine. Her normally jade eyes are dark, like the Amazonian forest. Her body is trembling and I'm practically holding her up by her neck. Her sweet juices soak my hand. "Come for me. Let that fucking pussy squirt." My menacing growl is feral and her body locks, her cunt clamps down, squeezing my fingers like a vise and I feel the honeyed cum dripping from her.

My cock has never been this hard. It's never throbbed so much to be inside a woman. To mark her. Watching her come apart under my touch is like heroin, and my body is buzzing with the high. My hand slips from her and I bring it to my mouth, tasting her from my fingers. *Delicious, fucking delectable.*

Her body straightens, but her knees are still wobbly. "Kael, you can't just expect me to—"

"Yes, I fucking can." Frustration courses through my veins. She needs to get over this because I want her. "Don't you see? I want you." She shakes her head and stalks past me. The scent of her sweetness is thick in the room, and I want to fuck her into submission. Like I did on our first night together.

"You can't want me. I'm not available. I don't...do exclusivity." Her words are fierce and fire blazes in her eyes.

"I want you to do it with me. I want to own you." The words come easily and she turns to me with her mouth agape. I've hit the nail on the fucking head. Surely she knows who I am. Surely she can see it in my eyes. I implore her with my gaze, but she looks away.

"What do you know about owning a woman?" Her indignant tone makes me chuckle. This woman challenges every fucking ounce of my restraint and sanity and I wouldn't have it any other way.

"Did you like when *he* owned you?" I spit the words and her gaze snaps to mine. "Did you like being a pet?" Meeting her glare, I see her falter at my question. Anger and hatred surge through me like venom, slowly poisoning me with the desire to exact revenge for her. To kill for her.

Her eyes shoot daggers at me. She lifts her chin and squares her shoulders. "If you're not here to watch me dance or fuck, then get out. I have work to do." She spins on her heel and grips the long steel pole that's nailed into the floor and ceiling in the center of the room. She twirls, watching me as she does, and I'd be lying if I said she wasn't distracting.

"You don't have work to do. I'm here. A client, paying for you." I stroll toward her, and she stops midair, legs wrapped around the metal and I wish I was the fucking pole.

"You're paying for my pussy? Right now, it seems you're not getting what you came for." Her retort is vicious. I'm up for a hate fuck if that's what she wants.

Halting, I lock my gaze on hers.

"Why don't you come down here and let me show you what it's like to be owned, Phoenix, because I'd like to show you how a real man treats his pet." The room is dimly lit, small low lights blink from the ceiling, allowing her eyes to glint like gemstones and I can't help but be hypnotized.

She slides down the pole in a teasing erotic dance, and I think I may have just come in my jeans.

Skyla

He wants to own me?

It's laughable. He comes across as a romantic, but he wants to *own* me. I stalk toward him in my five-inch heels. I noticed the bulge in his jeans ages ago, I stopped myself from gawking at it, but God I want to.

If he wants to play that game, then he can bring it on because I've got a fucking degree in it. I lean in and whisper in his ear. "What would you like to show me, *Sir?*" His body visibly trembles at the word, and I can't hide my smile. Stepping back, I meet his heated gaze, which scorches me from the tips of my toes to the top of my head.

"Kneel." His word comes out harshly—rough and demanding—and I obey. *Like I've been taught to.* "Do you have a collar, Phoenix?"

I nod. "Top drawer is mine." I point to the chest of drawers against the wall beside the door. I hear his footfalls, then the drawer of playthings opens and closes. The clink of metal echoes through the room and my body aches.

Each room has a chest of drawers, which allows us girls to store our toys. I've always kept a collar in each room because most of the clients who come in here want to tie me up. They want to play the Dom, so I indulge them, but only one man has ever owned me.

In the past, I would've been afraid, but somehow I know that Kael will not hurt me. He lowers to his haunches and latches the black and red collar around my neck. It's made of soft leather and the silver ring is attached to a leash of steel links.

"Come." The gruff tone of his voice is enough to get my panties wet, and I crawl behind him. He seats himself in the chair opposite the bed and tugs the chain so I'm kneeling between his thick muscled thighs. "Eyes up." My gaze latches on to his, finding fierce hunger boring into me. His index finger traces my chin, lifting my head. With the pad of this thumb, he swipes it over my lower lip. "Don't doubt this. I choose you, firebird. I want you as a woman, a submissive, a toy, not because you're weak, but because of your strength."

He stares at me for a long moment as if he's trying to pierce my soul, attempting to break down the walls I have surrounding me. I want to say something, but I don't because I don't want to break the spell. The memory that's so vivid in my mind.

"Undo my jeans. I want to watch that pretty little mouth swallow my dick." Without hesitation, I reach for the zipper I've been dying to touch since he walked in. Tugging his pants down along with his briefs, I salivate with need for that thick cock—rock hard and leaking with desire. Wrapping my fist around it, I stroke in slow measured movements, up and down until his free hand grips my hair. His face inches from mine. "Suck it, pet." His words are demanding and his eyes glower, but he's not angry.

He's not forcing me, he's commanding me.

I watch him relax against the charcoal-colored chair while my mouth engulfs the crown, tasting his salty sweetness on my tongue. I swirl, lick, and suck him—deeper and deeper—until I feel him hit the back of my throat. A low groan rumbles through his chest. My body is alight with every emotion I can think of, but the one that seems to burn brightest is need. I don't want this man. I fucking *need* him.

"That's it, baby." He opens his eyes and watches me intently. "Oh, God your mouth is perfect." Cupping his heavy balls in one hand, I squeeze, massaging them while I take him into my throat, so deep you'd be able to see the bulge in my neck.

Another growl from him spurs me on and I hum, sending the vibration down his dick and through his body. "Fuck!" Suddenly, without warning, jets of hot cum shoot into my mouth and down my throat. I pull my mouth off him and the hot saltiness hits my lips.

Black eyes hold me hostage, then he smiles. It's a wicked smirk that curls his lips in the sexiest way I've ever seen.

"You look beautiful with my cum on your face." He tugs the leash so I'm pulled forward, my face now closer to his. "Now it's my turn." He stands suddenly, yanking the collar. "On the bed." He drops the chain tethering me to him, and I quickly make my way onto the bed. "On your back, legs open."

I get in position and hear the rustling of his clothes.

"Please." The plea from my lips startles me. I've never begged. Ever. But as I watch him climb on the bed like a lion hunting his prey, I wonder what I'm actually asking for.

Sex? A fuck? Ownership?

Or something I've never thought I could have again. Love.

"Tell me what you want," he says, running his hands up my thighs. "Because you know what I want. There's no denying we fit together." He kneels between my legs, gripping the leash, tugging it toward him. Soft lips feather my own, "Tell me, Paige. Tell me we belong together." My body tenses. Nobody knows *that* name. It's been years since I've even heard it spoken.

"How the—" I push against him, but he doesn't relent. His body is too heavy on me and I can't move.

"I said tell me," he commands once more, and our

eyes meet, locked in a standoff, and all I want to do is submit. To give in to him and let go of the control I've had on my life, on my past. But then I want to argue, fight him and see how it is that he knows me. He grips my chin, forcing me to look at him. "Get out of your head. Let me in. Stop being so fucking stubborn," he growls, dragging me from my darkness and into his light. Pulling me from the fires of hell and showing me I may have risen from the ashes after all.

"Tell me how the fuck—"

His mouth crashes down on mine in a hard, unyielding kiss, searing me.

It's dominant and all consuming.

He's stealing my every breath with his lips and tongue. In return, he's breathing new life into me.

This man is taking my universe and fucking with it. Suddenly, he drives into me and I'm pushed into the mattress as he claims every inch of my body with his fingers, tongue, and cock.

"Kael," I manage to murmur when he finally breaks our kiss.

"It's your Wolfe, my little Red. My sweet Phoenix," he murmurs, and my world tilts, spins, and is knocked off its fucking axis. My head swirls, and as he thrusts into me, as we connect in the most primal way, he lifts his head, and when I look at him then, I finally see it. All doubt fades away. My heart stops, and when it kicks back to life and beats against my chest painfully I recognize him, his eyes, only his eyes.

"It is you," I whisper in shock and awe.

The truth startles me into complete submission, and all I can do is relent and let him take me.

His cock buried inside me, fully seated, filling me like only he can.

Not only claiming my body, but my heart, and soul.

The End... Or is it?

Are you ready to see what happens to Kael and Skyla?
Keep reading for an excerpt of Covet

PROLOGUE
Skyla

July 2015

It's been over a month since I was given to him. Almost six weeks of my life has been spent in the dark. With the only light being him.

"This is what you were born to do," he murmurs with conviction, with emotion, with everything he thinks I need. Those are the same things I now covet. When I'm alone in my room. When he's out somewhere, doing God knows what, it's him I think about. It's our time here in this darkened room that reminds me my life isn't what I'd planned it to be. In this chilly space, where it's me and him, I'm reminded that I was stolen. We're not a couple. Only Master and slave.

There are things he does to me that make me feel. I've fallen *down the rabbit hole and now I wish his actions meant more. He hides it so well. The emotion and affection. It's there beneath a cool exterior.*

The mask he wears reminds me of a predator.

A wolf.

The color of a raven's feathers—black as night, with a splash of crimson which could be the blood he draws from the lashes on my body. There's a deep-rooted anger in his dark eyes, but it's not aimed at me. Even though he enjoys taking it out on me, he never hurts me like I've heard the other trainers do to the girls.

Every time I meet his dark gaze, something human flickers behind it.

An outsider may think I'm crazy, and yes, I might be, but there's something caring about him. There have been many times in my training when he could have hurt me more than he has. But he's been…gentle. I suppose to most what I've been through is far from gentle. Does it make me a masochist to enjoy my caning? Does it make me crazy to enjoy when he makes me come after he's bound me and tortured my nipples and clit with clamps? Perhaps, but for my Wolfe, I'll do anything.

"Do you understand me?" he growls in my ear, but I don't respond. Like an animal, a real living and breathing feral dog. He's in my cage, and given half the chance, I know he'll devour me.

Before I was brought here, I never understood how women could want men to claim them. I didn't think there was anything sexy about it, but being claimed and owned by him makes me realize I want it. Suddenly, my leash is tugged, and I'm pulled to my feet.

"Look at me." The order renders me speechless. I know I must obey, so I do.

Our eyes lock in a searing gaze. There's nothing I can do but stare into dark orbs that remind me of cocoa. Such a conflicting range of feelings and emotions sweeps across the air between us like a tangible force—living and breathing between us.

"Do you know what you are?" he hisses, even though I feel no anger in the words. Just confusion, pain, and a deep-rooted agony that's stifling.

"Yes, Sir, I'm a slave." The words are ingrained inside me, deep in the core of my very being.

He leans in and my heart skitters. "Good girl," he murmurs, allowing his hot breath to fan over my ear. There's an innate need in his voice. Yes, men talk to me with desire and lust in their tone, but this…there's something different about him. The maelstrom of emotion that drips from his words hangs heavily in the air.

The first time he stalked into my room and laid his eyes on me, there was an innate connection between us. I noticed it, he did too, and our sessions took on a new set of rules.

As we spent our days together, I learned more about this predator. I've looked into his dark, anguish filled eyes and recognized the pain and guilt, but what stands out more than anything is the passion.

There was one poignant moment in our journey. When I knew he wanted more than we'd ever be allowed to have—the moment I bled, and he broke. Now I find myself at his mercy once more, waiting for the pain.

He rounds me, and the heat of his chest on my back has me

melting into his body.

I can't see his face, but I can feel him. As if he's rooted within me. Even though what we have may be detrimental, lethal, there's no denying it. He is my tormentor, my savior, my lover. And I'm his forbidden fruit. I belong to Wolfe when no one is around. I am owned.

He tugs the leash and walks into the room where we have our training. A room that has seen so many tears, heard so many words thrown in anger and hatred. He pulls me onto a bench I've never seen before, dragging me from the memories.

He binds me to the black leather bench in silence. My feet are cuffed to either side and my hands are bound in front of me. Face down on the scented leather, I wait.

The silence always comes before the pain.

The calm before the storm.

That's what he's taught me.

"Close your eyes, little one." This is our routine. He tells me not to look when he's about to do something difficult. Harsh even. When I know blood will be spilled, he tells me to shut my "pretty green eyes." And I do. My God, I do. The agony I know will follow is going to leave me lacerated.

A gentle feathering against my skin startles me, then the thin, sheer material I was wearing is gone. Another feather light touch and then it starts. A whip cuts into me harshly. I've been spanked, paddled, and flogged, but this sends me into another dimension. The sound that catapults from me is inhuman.

Another bite into my skin and another.

Whack! Whack!

Liquid oozes down my back. I can feel it trickling down like syrup drizzled over sweet treats. Nothing could ever prepare a person for something like this.

The agony. The pain. The torment.

But I don't beg for reprieve, I take it like he taught me. All I feel are the silent, salty emotions racing down my cheeks. Every time he does this—that we do this—it's different. The mood shifts, the emotions choke me. I want this, but only because it's him. I need this, because he's the one delivering the blows. And as my tears fall, they drip like a poison. But they won't kill me, as much as I wish they would, I'm still here. I'm still falling for a man who hurts me. And with every lash, with every sting, he soothes me where I need it most. He appeases my soul.

"Good girl. I'm proud of you," he murmurs, soft lips on mine. Those words. They seep into the wounds now scorching my back. He unlatches me, and I'm freed from my confines. Every move I make feels as if my skin is on fire. This isn't pain, this is so much more, so much worse. And as I meet my tormentor's stare, I realize this has hurt him as much as it did me. He doesn't realize how much his eyes tell me. How much they convey all the emotion he stores behind the mask. It's clear as day. Love.

I want to tell him to steal me away. I want to say so much in that moment, but I don't. We just stare each other down for a long while.

"You did well today, little one." His soothing tone eases the ache on my back. "Stay down, I need to see to these so they don't scar." He pushes me down roughly, and I obey. The cold balm he rubs into my wounds stings, but it also adds a sense of serenity. "Time to get some sleep, pet. You'll be busy tomorrow," he says and I can hear the pain in his words. Even though they calm me *in their own way, there's one confession I want from him which never comes.*

I want to ask more questions, but I know I'll never get my answers because that's not what he can offer me.

FIND COVET ON ALL MAJOR E-RETAILERS!

ACKNOWLEDGMENTS

Wow! This book. This novella. This damn story! It's been in the making for far too long. But now that it's in the hands of you amazing readers, I can breathe easy. All the love and support that you've shown for Skyla and Kael's novella has been humbling and I can't thank you enough.

When I created this couple, I didn't think it would spiral into a series at all. I wrote them, changed, then reworked them and as they say, third time's a charm.

This is an introduction to the Forbidden Series where you'll meet all the characters in full length novels. This isn't the last time you'll see Kael and his Phoenix.

I've had an integral team behind me. If they weren't there, pushing me to get this out, I don't think I would have hit publish on it.

In saying that, I'd like to first off thank my BETA babes—Kate, Danielle, Lisa, Kenzie, Kristina, Christina, Lizzie, Heather, Simone. If you ladies didn't show so much love for these characters, we wouldn't be here. Thank you!! <3

My editor, Vanessa and the PREMA team, thank you a million times over. Editing this story twice to make sure it's all polished and ready for the masses, you've made the story shine! Thank you!! <3

To my Street Team & my Dreamers, you ladies are incredible. I head to Facebook for a laugh and support, and you all offer that and so much more! Thank you!! <3

My IG #BookBabes, there are so many of you! I FLOVE you all!! Thank you for posting, reposting, commenting, and just general swooning over my alphas. Thank you!! <3

All the authors who share my posts, reposts, and offer support, you ladies are incredible. I don't know where I'd be without all of you. Thank you for being incredible women who I can look up to. <3

To the bloggers, you guys rock!! Thank you for your support, love, and hard work. It's not easy running a blog, but you all do it with no complaint. #AllBlogsMatter! FLOVE you!! <3

Last, but certainly not least, my readers. Each and every one of you are the reason I do this. When I get comments and DM's from all of you, I can't help but smile. Thank you!! <3

Also by Dani

Head to my website for a full list of my incredible titles

www.danirene.com

About Dani

Dani is a *USA Today* Bestselling Author of seductive and deviant romance.

Her books range from the dark to emotional, but every hero is alpha, and each heroine is strong-willed, bringing the men down to their knees.

She now lives in the UK, after moving from Cape Town, with her better half who does all the cooking while she writes all the words.

When she's not writing, she can be found binge-watching the latest TV series, or working on graphic design. She has a healthy addiction to reading, tattoos, coffee, and ice cream.

www.danirene.com | info@danirene.com